AN UNEXPECTED KISS

The door had scarcely closed behind Sir Perrick before William vented his anger. "Miss Addington, I am not certain what you were taught about proper behavior in Italy, but a young lady does not throw herself into the arms of a gentleman in such a vulgar fashion in England."

Startled by the unwarranted attack, Adriana sputtered, "My lord, you mistake what you saw."

"Did I, or are Roman manners quite different from proper ones? In Italy is a lady allowed to dispense her favors freely?"

What was he accusing her of? she wondered. She began to become quite angry. "I was merely thanking the gentleman for having returned my necklace, my lord, nothing more. It was Sir Perrick who tried to take advantage of the situation."

"Thanking him!" William's ire was so great, he took a step toward the lady. "Then why have you not thanked me in such a manner, for I am your escort to Scotland?"

With that, the gentleman suddenly pulled the lady into his arms and kissed her. . . .

Books by Lynn Collum

A GAME OF CHANCE
ELIZABETH AND THE MAJOR
THE SPY'S BRIDE
LADY MIRANDA'S MASQUERADE
AN UNLIKELY FATHER

Published by Zebra Books

THE CHRISTMAS CHARM

Lynn Collum

ZEBRA BOOKS
Kensington Publishing Corp.
http://www.zebrabooks.com

ZEBRA BOOKS are published by

Kensington Publishing Corp.
850 Third Avenue
New York, NY 10022

All Kensington titles, imprints and distributed lines are available at special quantity discounts for bulk purchases for sales promotion, premiums, fund raising, educational or institutional use.

Special book excerpts or customized printings can also be created to fit specific needs. For details, write or phone the office of the Kensington Special Sales Manager: Kensington Publishing Corp., 850 Third Avenue, New York, NY, 10022. Attn. Special Sales Department. Phone: 1-800-221-2647.

First Printing: December, 2000
10 9 8 7 6 5 4 3 2 1

Printed in the United States of America

Many thanks to the multilingual Elizabeth Grainger,
a generous writer and friend

Prologue

Rome, 1808

"Hai paura?" Amy Addington asked in flawless Italian while she sat at the table in the small rented room just off the Via Zanardelli. Only thirteen, she adored her brother but was curious about his feelings on this occasion. Alexander had just informed his sisters he must leave Rome that very night, his intended destination England.

He looked up from the list of things he needed to make certain he'd packed. Missing what his sister had said, he asked, *"Che dici?"*

"I asked if you were afraid."

"Afraid?" He uttered the word with all the youthful disdain he could muster. Like many young men who reach the age of sixteen, he believed in his invincibility. Life had yet to strip him of that illusion. "I am quite grown. I don't need Father or anyone else to accompany me to school."

Adriana, at fifteen the middle child of Hugh and Angelina Addington, stood at the table and sliced a loaf of bread for their invalid mother's tea tray. "But you are not merely going to school, Alex. You must go to escape the danger of being conscripted into the French Army, or worse should they discover you have English blood. They would throw us all into prison. I fear you won't be truly safe until Papa puts you on the ship to Greece. There is such danger." A chill of fear for her brother made Adriana shudder a bit. "You will be quite alone until our godmother, Lady Margaret, meets you in England. What if you become lost in Athens or miss your ship at some other port of call?"

The young man with a startlingly handsome countenance and dark, unruly locks shrugged his shoulders as if the danger affected him little. He walked to the window of the *pensione* and gazed out at the Ponte Sant'Angelo, which crossed the Tiber in the distance. "I shan't lose my way. I'm looking forward to the journey. In truth, I worry more about the family still here under French rule. If only Mama could travel, and we might go together . . ."

Adriana laid the knife down and went to stand beside Alexander. She knew he was torn about leaving them behind and wished to reassure him. "We'll be quite safe here in Roma. The danger was in Firenze, where everyone knew of our English blood. Besides, Papa will take care of us as he always has. And if Mama's health improves, we might yet join you in London. Would it not be nice to meet Papa's family at long last?"

Alex grinned down at his sister. "You cannot fool me. You care nothing of our English relations, who have mostly ignored us all these years. Since Lady Weldon told you and Amy that you would be Diamonds of the First Water with your dark eyes and locks, you have been dreaming of a London Season."

Amy left her chair and joined her siblings at the window, having followed the conversation. "But don't you see, Alex? Here nearly everyone is a dark beauty, but in London Ana and I would be quite unique."

Alex chucked his little sister under the chin. "Then when I am eighteen I shall purchase a pair of colors in the British army and help defeat the French in time for my sisters to journey across the seas and dazzle London's Society, little one."

The youngest Addington snorted. "You have always wanted to be a soldier, so don't try to convince us that you will be joining the army for us. And just where are *you* planning to get funds to purchase a pair of colors?"

Alex waggled his brows. "You don't actually think I'm going to school to study, do you? I shall game my way through the halls of Eton and pluck those little lords clean just like Father does with the local gentlemen."

"Ha, I'm much better at whist than you," Amy boasted, putting her hands upon her hips. "I should—" The sound of their mother's bell ringing in the depths of the inn caused the youngest to turn and listen. Then she patted her elder sister's arm maternally. "I shall take Mama her tea since you walked to the piazza to buy the bread."

With that, Amy hurried to the fire and took the kettle from the spit. At the table she set the plate of sliced bread on a wooden tray along with the pot of hot water as well as a bottle of wine and olive oil. Their mother had developed many English habits over the years of her marriage to Hugh Addington, but she was Italian after all.

Alexander opened the door for Amy, then returned to the window where Adriana had remained watching the dwindling passersby in the fading light, her mood somber. The air held the familiar scent of garlic, sausage, olives, and the damp river. They stood in silence for a moment, savoring the sight, then he gave his sister a sheepish glance.

"I'm glad we have this moment alone. I wanted to find something for both you and Amy since I might not see you again until you are grown . . . but I hadn't the funds for two proper gifts, so I compromised."

Surprised at such sentimentality from a brother more likely to tease them than to show affection, Adriana fought back tears as Alexander reached into his pocket and drew out a small black box. He thrust it awkwardly into his sister's hand.

"Since I cannot be here to watch over you, I bought a medallion that the man said was blessed by the pope himself before the French seized him and took him from Roma."

"But we aren't Catholic and Papa would not approve."

Alexander waved his hand. " 'Tis nothing religious, just an old Roman goddess. I'm giving it to you for good luck."

She opened the box and discovered a necklace with a small gold medallion engraved with a woman, laurel leaves encircling her head. Dressed in a coat of mail, the female held the great sword of a warrior. Adriana looked up at her brother and smiled. "Am I to be the family dragon slayer in your stead?"

"You would be a good one, but I fear there are no dragons left to slay. The engraving is the goddess Minerva, quite a favorite here in Roma. Look at the back of the charm."

Adriana turned the medallion over and discovered Latin symbols. She arched one brow. "What does it say?"

" 'Wisdom and prudence.' " Alex awkwardly took his sister's hands. "Since I must go, I want you to wear this until you find your heart's desire. And when you discover what will make you happy, pass the necklace on to Amy so that it will bring the luck she needs to find what she truly wants."

Adriana's throat tightened and she blinked back tears. She threw her arms around her brother's neck and hugged him. "We shall miss you dreadfully, but I know this is what you have always desired."

The door to the small sitting room opened as the brother and sister drew apart. Hugh Addington, his brown hair several shades lighter than his children's, looked sadly at his only son. While it remained unspoken, they all knew years would pass before they would again see each other. In softly spoken English, he said, "Come bid your mother good-bye, Alexander."

The siblings embraced one last time, then Adriana turned back to the window, staring at the Tiber River below with unseeing eyes welling with tears. She wondered if all sisters felt this wrenching emotion when their elder brothers left home for the first time. Or was it the strangeness of their situation?

The three of them had always been torn between the two cultures of their parents. Born in Italy of an Italian mother and an English father, they spoke both Italian and English with ease. They'd lived in comfort in a villa in the hills outside Firenze thanks to their grandfather, Conte Orsini, but their life had been much involved with the small, ever-changing English community. Papa's fellow countrymen flocked to Florence, as the British called the Town, for the weather and to purchase works of art.

That is, until Napoleon's army invaded northern Italy in 1799. Most of the English fled in front of the advancing French, but due to Angelina Addington's health, they had gotten only as far as Roma before realizing they could go no farther. For safety they'd assumed the Italian surname Accardi and settled into quiet obscurity in a *pensione* beside the Tiber.

But since the first of the year French troops occupied the city, and word quickly spread that young men were being conscripted. The hard decision to at last send Alexander to England had been unavoidable.

Adriana sighed. Despite her best efforts, envy filled her that her brother would at last see England. Sailing the seas, then seeing a new land, stirred her blood. Too long limited to these few rooms and the occasional trip to the piazza or the countryside, she'd grown restless.

Just then the door opened and Amy returned. She joined her sister at the window, propping her chin upon one hand, a wistful expression on her face. "Whatever shall we do without Alex to amuse us?"

"Oh, we are quite resourceful. I am certain our drawing and sewing will keep us tolerably amused. Look, there they go." The girls waved farewell to their father and brother as they climbed into the hired carriage.

"What have you in your hand?" Amy brushed the tears from her cheeks to see better the dangling ends of the delicate chain.

" 'Tis from Alex for both of us. I am to wear it first to give me wisdom as well as prudence. It's for luck, and when I find my heart's desire, I am to pass it along to you."

"A good luck charm!" Amy grinned. "Let me put it on you." She took the necklace and draped it around her sister's neck, then stood back and admired the medallion. "It is very pretty, but do you know what your heart's desire is?"

With a shake of her head, Adriana said, "Not yet, but I mustn't rush such an important decision. I have had it on for only a moment, so I am sure more wisdom will come the longer I wear it. See, I am exhibiting prudence already."

Amy laughed and the girls leaned out to wave at Alexander one last time. *"Ciao, Alessandro."*

Alex leaned out the coach window. Taking his beaver hat in hand, he waved it in the air. *"Arrivederci, mie bellissime sorèlle!"*

One

A line of gray-liveried servants carrying domed silver trays entered Lady Margaret, Dowager Countess of Wotherford's Berkeley Square dining room. Her ladyship's butler stood beside his mistress, eyeing the procession critically, his bushy gray brows drawn together. Without a single break in stride, every other footman went in the opposite direction, dividing and filing beside the long table of guests. At last each of the countess's company had a footman standing behind them.

As Baxter lifted his hand, about to signal for his underlings to place the next course before the gathered guests, another of the countess's servants slipped into the room from the main hall and whispered into the butler's ear. The austere old man with thinning gray hair flicked his head in a gesture of dismissal to the lone footman. With a graceful sweep downward of his hand, he signaled the waiting servants to set trays upon the table. The footmen swished away the silver domes to reveal glazed capons and herb-roasted potatoes.

Baxter leaned down and whispered into Lady Margaret's ear. Just as Mr. Thaddeus Wilcox grabbed fork and knife and eyed this new course with relish, the countess gasped, then cried, "They're alive!"

Mr. Wilcox frowned and peered from his capon to the

countess's own cooked bird. He could see no difference. "I do assure you, my lady, they are not alive. They are roasted to a turn."

Lady Margaret waved her hands. "I do not mean these hens, Thaddeus, I am referring to my goddaughters who have been stranded in Italy since that monster Napoleon has been on the loose."

Lady Alice, sitting opposite Mr. Wilcox, frowned. "Why did they not leave when the dreadful fellow was exiled the first time?"

"Their father hasn't been well since the death of his wife. They, like the rest of us, thought we'd seen the last of the Little Corsican after he was sent to Elba."

Mr. Wilcox, caring little about these unknown people foolish enough to gad about on the continent, again raised his knife and fork. "Well, I think we have seen the last of the fellow now that he's been sent to St. Helena." With sheer delight, he sliced into the capon.

The Countess of Wotherford rose, speaking to her guests. "Pray enjoy your meal. I have a visitor with important news that I must see at once." Without further explanation, the countess followed her butler out of the dining room, where speculation ran rife as to what could be so important to draw her ladyship, a noted hostess, from her party.

Lady Margaret followed Baxter at an ambling gait, her sixty-nine years having slowed her a bit physically but not socially. She still greatly enjoyed her position as one of the premier hostesses of the *ton*. "Where did Ben put Mrs. Reed?"

"In the library, my lady."

The butler opened the door and Lady Margaret, full of questions, swept into the room. "What news of Hugh and the girls, Vivian? Are they well? Do they intend returning to England at long last?"

Mrs. Vivian Reed, younger sister of Mr. Addington,

seated before the unlit fireplace, dressed in a lavish black gown despite the fact that her husband had been dead these past two years. The lady was as tall as most men, with a mannish, rawboned appearance that always startled Lady Margaret, since as a general rule the Addingtons were a handsome family.

"I fear the news is not what we would have wished. My brother is dead these last six months and the girls are without enough funds to travel to England."

Lady Margaret sat heavily on the opposite leather chair. She'd had an uncommon fondness for Hugh Addington. His mother had been Margaret's best friend at seminary and it had always been their desire that Hugh would marry the countess's daughter, Iris. But the late Lord Wotherford had objected, so Iris had wed the wealthy Viscount Borland instead of Hugh, merely the distant heir to a barony whose livelihood had been derived from his skill with cards.

Lady Margaret could not deny she would miss seeing Hugh again, but at the moment the most important matter involved bringing Adriana and Amy home from Italy. She was certain that would be what Alexander would have wished. He had spoken of it during his short stay with her in 1808 and in each new missive since.

"Have you responded to their letter? Invited them to come? Sent them funds?" Lady Margaret, a woman of action, had little patience for indecision.

Mrs. Reed primly folded her hands in her lap. "I have not. As much as I should like to, my solicitor tells me I cannot afford to bring two young ladies from Italy and house them indefinitely. I have a daughter to present this coming spring. My circumstances do not allow for such extravagance, my lady. That is why I have come to you. I knew that you were in communication with their brother, and I hoped he might provide the funds."

The countess suspected the lady exaggerated her situation, for Mrs. Reed's late husband had been a successful barrister, but Lady Margaret wasn't going to stand about and quibble over money. "Alexander is currently with the occupation army in northern France. But I shall stand the expense and invite the Addington girls to come and stay with me."

Vivian Reed opened her reticule, then handed the letter she withdrew to the countess. "They are adamant that they do not wish charity, my lady. Adriana writes that they will stay with me only long enough to obtain employment."

This was a leveler for Lady Margaret. She'd recently made plans that involved Miss Adriana Addington after receiving a letter from Alexander after Waterloo. He wanted her to help bring his family to London. He'd even offered to send her the funds when the arrangements were made.

It had been Major Addington who'd given her the idea about his sister, albeit inadvertently. On the very day he'd first arrived in England so many years before, he'd shown his godmother two miniatures of his sisters, and their beauty even at such tender ages had struck the countess. But it hadn't been until the previous week when she'd again heard disturbing rumors about Randolph Jamison, her grandson's heir, that she realized she must do something. Lord Borland must produce an heir he could be proud of, and not leave the estate to a loose fish like Randolph.

The countess knew her grandson, the present Viscount Borland, and Adriana would be a perfect match, for he was brilliant and she beautiful. But how to bring the two of them together if the girl insisted on finding employment once she reached England?

Mrs. Reed cleared her throat. When Lady Margaret looked up, Vivian leaned forward, a speculative gleam in her brown eyes. "I have a suggestion that might suit us both. If you can provide the funds to bring my nieces to England, we might each employ one of the girls. The eldest could be a companion for you, the youngest a companion for my daughter, Helen. That would be far better than having them working for strangers."

As the countess suspected, Mrs. Reed's circumstances weren't as dire as she'd intimated, or did the pinch-purse intend to use the younger Miss Addington as an unpaid servant as so many did with poor relations? For the moment, the countess wouldn't worry about Amy since she felt certain Mrs. Reed would not ill treat the girl even if she didn't fairly compensate her.

Lady Margaret rose and went to her desk. "How soon can you have them in England?"

"I had my husband's former partner inquire. If I send them funds and tickets at once, they could be in Plymouth by the first of December."

That would be perfect. Lady Margaret opened the desk drawer and drew out a small strongbox. She pulled out a pouch full of coins and handed it to Mrs. Reed. "That should take care of all expenses. Have the girls come to you in Basingstoke and I shall send a maid for Adriana. I want her to be at Wother Castle in time for Christmas."

Mrs. Reed seemed to weigh the pouch for a moment before she stowed it in her reticule. Then the lady frowned as the countess's words seemed to penetrate her thoughts. "You intend for Adriana to travel all the way to Scotland with only a maid?"

"Why, no. She need travel only so far as London. I shall make other arrangements after that. Now, you must excuse me, for I have guests." She escorted Mrs. Reed to the library door, where Baxter waited to show the lady out.

But the countess did not return to her guests. Instead, she went to the desk and sat down, her mind whirling with ideas. Should she wait for the girl in London, then take her to William's estate? Shaking her head, she realized it was likely he would merely retreat to his library and they would rarely see him.

What she needed was a situation that would require William to spend time with Miss Addington. Then the idea struck her. She could have her grandson escort Adriana to Kelso for Christmas. That way he would have to come for her traditional Christmas party. Still, the countess wondered, if she returned to Scotland, how could she coax him to London at just the right moment? And if he did accompany Adriana, would anything come from their long journey together?

After some thought she realized that if nothing came of his meeting with the young lady, at least he wouldn't be stuck in his library, his nose in a dusty book. And she would have him at the castle for the holidays. But how the devil was she going to lure William away from his Yorkshire estate to do her bidding?

The butler returned from having escorted Mrs. Reed out. "Your guests are waiting, my lady."

"Baxter, I need my grandson in London by the first of December. What trick will entice him here, for you know an invitation from me won't suffice? He's already turned down my request he come to Kelso for Christmas."

Baxter had been in Lady Margaret's employ some forty years and didn't find her plotting the least surprising. "Why, my lady, I do believe the only reason he comes to London these days is when that book dealer he frequents has something unusual for him."

The lady's blue eyes glowed. "You are correct. What is that book fellow's name?"

"He's foreign, I believe. Shall I make inquiries?"

"At once, Baxter. I want to see that man here before the week's end. He shall have three months to find something rare enough to entice William to Town."

Lady Margaret exited the library to return to her guests, convinced that with a bit of inventiveness she might yet have her stubborn grandson wed to Miss Addington and fulfill her wish. That he hadn't any desire for a wife bothered her not the least.

Some three weeks later, to the surprise of her many friends, the knocker was removed from the door of Lady Margaret's Berkeley Square town house. She set out north during the height of the Little Season, having sent her regrets to all the entertainments to which she'd been invited. Well satisfied with the plans in place for the arrival of Adriana Addington, she nearly purred with satisfaction as her coach rumbled up the North Road. All she needed was news that the girl had arrived in Basingstoke, and her plans would be set in motion.

One last task remained, and that entailed a visit to her grandson's estate near Sheffield. No doubt he would be less than delighted to see her, since the last time they were together they had quarreled over his obstinate refusal to come to London for the Season in the spring. But she had some information she needed to impart that might at least spur the viscount to consider the possibility of a bride.

In many ways Lady Margaret's own daughter was to blame for William's reluctance to marry. Having been widowed when her son was but five years old, Iris had been terrified something might happen to her only child and had kept him close to her. She discouraged any activity she felt dangerous. Reading, art, and music with well-paid instructors made the boy scholarly and creative but without companions his own age, he soon became a man in a child's body. Any thoughts of play or pranks by the boy were quickly stifled by Iris.

Lady Margaret intervened when the boy turned eleven,

insisting that all young gentlemen must ride, drive a carriage, and go to school. Iris wept and worried but at last relented to riding and driving lessons. As to school, she declared Eton could never provide the superior instruction he received at Borwood Abbey.

Despite his cosseting, William, fifth Viscount Borland, had grown into a strong, athletic young man who proved to be a good manager of his estate when the family solicitor had turned over the reins at eighteen. But in Lady Margaret's opinion, he was too bookish and too content to live quietly out of Society. It was no doubt the result of the excessive demands of his mother as her failing health worsened that made William seek peace and serenity in his current life.

Hoping to set her grandson on a new path after his mother's death, Lady Margaret suggested he go away to school, as most titled young men did. So he consented to his grandmother's wishes and did a year at Oxford. But the viscount declared to his grandmother that the dons had little to offer that he couldn't find in his own extensive library.

Life in school was difficult for the serious young man. He had little in common with the frivolous young men more interested in gaming and wenching than in their studies. Save a few scholarly schoolmates, William found little to his taste and soon returned to Sheffield.

When he turned five and twenty, his grandmother again descended on his estate, convincing him he must come to London and find a wife to secure the Jamison line. But his foray into the social world had proven an even greater disaster than his academic life. He'd found the ladies of Society, from young to old, to be as emptyheaded as the stone griffins that graced the gates in front of Borwood Abbey. Yet even as he'd failed to encourage a single female, they'd pursued him unmercifully.

While at Oxford he'd discovered females had their

uses, but outside of bed they had little to hold his interest. The one bright spot of his single Season had been his discovery of Signor Fiorette, a dealer in rare books and paintings.

Undaunted by her failed efforts, Lady Margaret tried each spring to entice her grandson to Town with her, but he always patiently reminded her that he was content with his life at the abbey. He didn't want some female chattering inanities at him all day, disturbing his peace. He also politely reminded her that he had an heir in his young cousin, Mr. Randolph Jamison.

Since Baxter had given her Signor Fiorette's name, her new plans were ready to set in motion. Lady Margaret had happily departed for Yorkshire. Two days after the countess had set out from London, her carriage bowled up the drive to Borwood Abbey. She'd rehearsed her speech throughout the journey. Some of her friends might consider her interfering, but she wanted only that her grandson realize there was an entire world outside the confines of a book and his estate.

Upon entering his lordship's library, the expression on her grandson's handsome face spoke volumes. As usual, the room was cluttered, every table stacked with a variety of books ranging from large tomes to small treatises.

"Grandmother, I didn't expect to see you before December, when you make your usual journey back to Scotland for Christmas." He rose reluctantly from in front of the small fire, then seemed to search behind her. "Where is the faithful Boris?"

"He's not with me. The old fellow doesn't like London, but 'tis nice that you have come to worry about him at last."

"Actually, I still think him little more than an exotic flea transport, but I know you have a great affection for him."

"I blame your mother for your dislike of animals indoors, always prattling that they might carry some disease." Lady Margaret came forward, and her grandson kissed her, then she took a seat before she added, "And Boris doesn't have a flea on him. I wouldn't allow anything so common."

"To be sure." The viscount decided not to contradict the lady by informing her about the sorry state of the rugs in her bedchamber after her last visit with the wolfhound.

Grandmother and grandson exchanged a smile that held a hint of a challenge, then she asked, "What were you reading so intently, dear boy?"

William closed the book in his hand. "Sir Robert Hawkins's book, *Observations of His Voyages of the South Sea.* Nothing that would interest you, I'm certain."

The countess smoothed her travel-wrinkled gown, then looked back at William. "I see you are still living your life through the adventures of others."

The viscount's brow wrinkled. "I would hardly call an interest in learning about the world living my life through others. Contrary to what you believe about me, I have a great deal to handle here every day, Grandmother."

The lady sighed, knowing she wouldn't accomplish her mission if she quarreled with her grandson again. "I have no doubt, dear boy. I haven't come to criticize you. I am merely on my way back to Scotland and wanted to spend a few days here with you and rest before continuing. I'm not as young as I used to be."

William eyed his grandmother closely. She looked as robust as usual in a maroon traveling gown trimmed with white swansdown, her cheeks only moderately lined despite her advanced age. "I have never known you to leave London before the end of November. Is there some problem?"

"I must go home and see how Boris is doing. Mrs. Lynley wrote to say the old fellow is off his feed."

"You are going all the way back to Scotland because your dog is a bit out of curl?" William asked skeptically.

"He is not just *a* dog, but a gift from Prince Igor Ivanovich on the earl's last visit to St. Petersburg. But as to my returning home, I daresay, I am merely too old for all the rigors of Society." The lady gave another exaggerated sigh. "Or mayhap I simply couldn't face my friends when those dreadful rumors began to circulate."

"Rumors? Have you been naughty *again?*" William teased.

"Don't be ridiculous. I wasn't naughty even when I was younger. Naughty is vulgar. 'Tis you who should be concerned." She paused dramatically, then asked, "Do you know what they are calling your heir?"

"Oh, I am certain you have gleefully driven all this way to inform me." William resisted the urge to smile at her obvious ploy. His grandmother remained persistent in her attempt to persuade him to marry, her most recent gambit being the unsuitability of his heir.

"They are calling him Randy Randolph. There are no less than three notorious females under his protection at this moment, though how he can afford it, I cannot say. He even had the audacity to bring one of the creatures to the Miltons' masquerade dressed as a vestal virgin."

William quirked a half-smile. "I am quite amazed that a Lothario such as Randolph gave a thought to virgins, vestal or otherwise."

"This is nothing to laugh about, William. Randolph is no longer accepted in the best homes. People whisper that you are still young and likely to cut him out of the succession. They don't want to risk their daughters on such as he. While I have come to accept that you no longer wish to continue the line"—the countess prayed that God wouldn't strike her dead for that falsehood. Then when no bolt streaked from the heavens, she continued—"what kind of lady do you think your heir can procure for a bride if he rubs elbows only with such low females?"

The viscount rose and placed the book he held on the mantel, then turned to face his visitor. They'd had this discussion so many times that his patience was beginning to wear thin. "Randolph is scarcely five and twenty, madam. Like most, he will make many mistakes while he sows his oats. True, he may be a bit excessive, but he does nothing that many young cawkers don't do upon first being set loose on Society."

Lady Margaret stood, shaking her head. "For a man with such a great deal of knowledge in his head, you know little about people. He has had plenty of time to settle down, and yet he continues his wild lifestyle. Has it not occurred to you that without the guiding hand of a father, the fellow may never learn to exercise restraint? That his wicked ways are now set as they will always be?"

With those words, her ladyship made for the door, but once there, she paused, looking back at her grandson. "When that young man disgraces us all, don't say I didn't warn you. Now I shall go to my room to rest before dinner."

As the door closed behind Lady Margaret, William impatiently grabbed the book he'd been reading from the mantel and again settled into his chair. But he didn't open it. Instead, he gazed into the flames. Was his grandmother right? Was his cousin too far down the road of dissipation to marry a proper female and secure the Jamison line? Or was this just another of the countess's tricks to force her only grandson to marry one of those brainless females that littered the *ton?*

William ran his hand through his hair, turning sandy-brown waves into loose curls. How could *he* criticize his young cousin when he'd allowed his own wishes for peace and order in his home to stand in the way of doing his own duty to produce an heir?

It seemed to him he'd had more than his fair share of females trying to manage his life. First his mother, with all her unwarranted fears and demands, then his grandmother and her matchmaking. No longer could anyone control him with tears, ill health, or reminders of his duty.

Still, of late he'd found himself a bit restless as he sat beside the fire of an evening. His steward, who used to keep him company after supper to discuss the estate and politics, had recently retired and as yet hadn't been replaced. Then there was his neighbor, Sir Perry. Theirs was a strange friendship, having met after they were grown and having little in common. Still, they enjoyed each other's company. But William rarely saw Perry since the baronet spent a great deal more time in London raking and gaming than in Yorkshire.

Even William's closest friend from Oxford, Jonas Brand, a scholar and noted botanist, had married in the spring, leaving William feeling somewhat adrift. How had his friend managed to find a woman whose silly giggling and prattling didn't drive him to distraction? Or had he simply decided to tolerate the lady in order to have someone to manage his household and produce sons? It was all a mystery to him.

Opening the book, the viscount put his worries about the future aside. He had an excellent housekeeper and an acceptable heir. He had no intentions of bringing some female into his home who would likely disturb his quiet study. That was all there was to it.

"I leave in the morning!" Adriana spoke in Italian as she opened the door to the room she'd shared for the past week with her sister at her aunt Vivian's elegant house on the outskirts of Basingstoke. While the girls spoke perfect English, their mother's language seemed so much more comfortable when the two were alone. Their journey from Italy had been accomplished in too short a time in Adriana's thinking, but Amy had been more than delighted to set foot on the docks in Plymouth. Ships and sailing hadn't agreed with the youngest Addington lady.

Amy's expression grew bleak. "So soon, Ana? I'd hoped that we might have a chance to see the local countryside together before Lady Margaret sent for you." The young woman rose and went to embrace her sister.

They'd been through a great deal together, especially since the death of their mother. The familiar rooms of the *pensione* beside the Tiber had given way to a series of dirty inns over the years, until at last the sisters had come to share a single chamber on the outskirts of Rome after their father's death. Money had been tight and save for Adriana's skill with her sketching, and Amy's with a needle, they would have starved.

Adriana lifted the portmanteau Mrs. Reed had loaned her, insisting it was better for travel than the trunk she shared with her sister. Taking her sketch pads and pencils from atop the small writing desk, Adriana began the task of packing.

Watching her sister move to the wardrobe and begin to toss clothes into the small case without regard to wrinkles, Amy sank on the bed. "Ana, I cannot bear that we are no longer to be together."

Adriana ceased her careless packing and went to her sister. Sitting beside Amy on the lacy white counterpane, she placed a comforting arm about the younger girl's shoulders. "My dear, we have always known the time would come when we would have to go our own paths, as did Alexander. Don't you see, Aunt Vivian intends you to share in Cousin Helen's Season as her companion."

Amy clutched at her sister's hand. " 'Tis you I'm concerned about. To be a companion to an elderly lady in some dreadful Scottish castle is too bad. For you, who always wanted travel and adventure, it will not do. I shall go in your stead and you must stay with our aunt and Cousin Helen."

Patting her sister's hand, Adriana shook her head, causing her thick black curls to bounce. "No, indeed. You are the beauty and more likely to catch the eye of some gentleman who won't care a fig about our lack of dowry. After you are well married you might rescue me from lonely isolation, but in truth, my dear, after years in those inns, I long for a spacious castle with woods to roam and draw. That will be quite enough adventure for me. At least until Alexander returns to England. Then I should like to follow the drum with him. 'Tis you who have longed for your own home and hearth all these years."

The sisters sat staring at each other, knowing the truth in Adriana's statement. Amy, only twenty, was the classic beauty with dark, liquid eyes, raven-black curls, and full rose lips. She attracted attention wherever she went. She was small in stature but owned a well-formed figure. Her one true ambition was to find a real home instead of the cloistered life in the variety of *pensioni* they'd known since leaving their late grandfather's villa.

At two and twenty, the eldest Miss Addington stood nearly five feet nine in her stocking feet. She possessed her mother's black locks and dark eyes, but her mouth was a trifle wide and her slightly olive skin contrasted with her sister's ivory cheeks. Most people considered her handsome, but her beauty paled beside Amy's, a fact Adriana had long before accepted.

Being the eldest daughter, she'd been the primary caretaker of their mother, then later of their father. With those responsibilities lifted from her shoulders, she longed to be out experiencing life's great adventures, as Alexander was doing.

Amy knew this, but still she worried about her sister's fate. "You don't dislike the idea of being Lady Margaret's companion?"

"If she is anything like Alexander described in the first letter we managed to receive after he reached England, I don't think my life will be fetching fans, sewing, or reading boring sermons to a withered old lady. In fact, I think the eccentric Countess of Wotherford and I might be well suited. Do you not?"

Amy and Adriana laughed at the memory of the tale their brother had written about his godmother. The lady had arrived in Plymouth to greet his ship in a barouche, a great hairy dog that had been a gift from a Russian prince beside her. The animal had been dressed in a cossack-style cape and hat. In truth, the countess their brother described seemed to be a lady who was anything but the traditional Englishwoman.

"Perhaps you are right. And surely we shall see each other during the Season. Aunt Vivian says the countess never misses a single crush."

Adriana rose, her gaze again on the wardrobe. "I must finish packing—"

Amy put a restraining hand on her sister's arm, then pulled the jumbled garments from the portmanteau. "From the looks of things, I think I should do the packing. Do go bid Helen farewell, for I doubt she will be up in time to see you and Lady Margaret's maid off in the morning."

Adriana nodded. "Very well." She went to the door, then stopped, looking back at her younger sister. "Do you think you will like being Helen's companion?"

Amy stopped her folding, a thoughtful expression in her golden brown eyes. Then she gave a nod of her head. "Our cousin is quite a beauty and greatly spoiled by Aunt

Vivian. Worse, with Helen's love of novels I fear her head is full of foolish notions of fleeing to Gretna Green with some nameless duke, but I think there is no true vice in her."

"And if you should find her not as you think her?"

Amy grinned. "Then I will help her pack *her* bag to run away with her imaginary beaus."

Adriana laughed, then went to bid her cousin goodbye. She knew her sister was only teasing, for there were few people with as much calm good sense as Amy. Adriana had always been the one more likely to act on impulse.

As she went down the hall, her mood became more sober. In truth, she was more fearful than she'd told her sister about what she expected to find with Lady Margaret. Nancy, the maid sent to accompany her, had been full of her ladyship's praises, but Adriana put that down to a servant's loyalty. Would the lady have notions about how proper young ladies should behave and not allow Adriana the freedom of movement she desired?

She arrived at her cousin's door, thoughts about her future set aside. After a quick farewell with the young lady who seemed far more concerned with having her hair done up in papers than bidding her newly met relation a safe journey, Adriana returned to her room to discover everything all packed and ready.

In the predawn light the following morning, Aunt Vivian and Amy stood beside the hired post chaise as Adriana stepped inside to join Nancy. After the door was closed, Miss Addington lowered the window. "Thank you for all you have done for Amy and me, Aunt."

Mrs. Reed, looking more gaunt than usual in a voluminous gray mantle, kindly patted her niece's hand. "How could I leave my brother's children stranded in a foreign land? I am most glad to have you home and only wish I could have kept you both here."

Amy and Adriana exchanged a knowing look, since they felt everything in England was foreign and not home at all. Just then the carriage jerked forward. Adriana leaned out the window, waving. "I shall write when I reach Scotland. Good-bye, Aunt Vivian, good-bye, dearest Amy."

Adriana could see the tears in her sister's eyes that matched her own, and it had been much the same when they had parted from Alexander so long before. Still, she had no fears for her sister's welfare and comfort, for their aunt had been most welcoming to the two nieces she'd never before met.

Adriana continued to wave, leaning farther out until she could no longer see her dear sister as the post chaise rounded a turn in the road. A hand grabbed the back of her woolen cape and tugged her back into the coach.

"Sit yourself down, Miss Addington, afore you topple out on your head. What would I tell the countess then?" Nancy, like many old family retainers, had a motherly quality despite her youthful appearance. Adriana found she quite liked the maid.

"You needn't worry. Papa always said I was too hardheaded for my own good, so I doubt I would not be hurt. How long until we reach London?"

"We must make an overnight stop but should be in Portman Square by early in the morning on the morrow."

"I cannot wait to meet Lady Margaret."

The maid's face took on a rather pinkish hue. "Well, as to that, her ladyship is still in Scotland."

Disappointment raced through Adriana. She'd been hoping to meet her new employer and godmother within the next day or so. "Then 'tis just you and I traveling to Scotland."

Nancy made a great show of finding a handkerchief in her reticule. "No, miss, we are to be accompanied by her ladyship's grandson."

Adriana's eyes widened. "Is her ladyship unwell?"

"Why, no, miss, but she thought it a bit too much for her to ride all the way from Scotland and back in time to make all the arrangements for her Christmas party. And after all, his lordship was in Town and she was wantin' him to come to Kelso. So things worked out perfectly."

Something didn't seem quite in taking with all Adriana had heard of Lady Margaret. Or did this have more to do with the countess's grandson? She turned to the sturdy maid with the rosy cheeks beside her. "Pray, tell me about this gentleman."

With that the maid did exactly as she had been instructed by Lady Margaret, giving Miss Addington only the barest of details about the viscount. It wouldn't do to have the young lady set against the viscount before they'd even met.

Two

Viscount Borland shrugged into the dark blue superfine coat that his ancient valet held. But before the servant could do his usual inspection to make certain that the garment didn't pucker in some spot or that not a single speck of lint clung to the dark fabric, his lordship was for the door.

"Fiorette is due any moment, and I cannot wait to see what books he has found me. His message was intriguing."

The old servant, having served the viscount since the gentleman first donned long pants, halted his master. "Would that you were as excited about a proper young lady as you are that foreign book peddler."

William arched one brow as the valet came around and gently tugged the tails of his coat to smooth the lines in the back. "You begin to sound like a matchmaking old woman, Clayton."

"No need to be insultin', my lord. It's just the staff would love to hear the sounds of children at the abbey," the valet remarked even as his gaze diligently raked the gentleman's garment for flecks of white. After all, he did have his reputation to consider, and they were in London, where servants gossiped unmercifully about one another.

"Just what I want, screeching children to disrupt the quiet of my library."

Clayton picked up the viscount's discarded banyan

from the chair even as he remarked, "But what good is all that knowledge you've acquired, my lord, if you don't impart it to someone, and who better than your own offspring?"

"I am too set in my ways at two and thirty. The staff will have to wait until Randolph fills the nursery with children."

"Well, if you don't mind the next generation of Jamisons being addlepated, whey-faced monkeys like your nephew, who am I to object?"

"Who indeed?" William chuckled as he exited his chamber in Portman Square in high spirits. It was in truth unfortunate that Randolph did resemble a simian with his excess of dark hair, stooped shoulders, and long arms, but there was little one could do about such family traits. Lord Borland put the matter from his mind, instead pondering what Fiorette might have found him.

Despite Clayton's impertinence, there seemed to be nothing that would disturb the viscount's visit to London this time. His grandmother was safely ensconced in her castle in Kelso, and not likely to land on his doorstep to badger him into going to some boring entertainment as was her usual trick each time he ventured to Town.

The viscount had just reached the first landing when the knocker sounded, echoing through the hall. He paused and waited in anticipation as his London butler strolled to the door without the least hurry. The portal opened and there stood the short, round book dealer with two men holding a trunk behind him.

Seeing his lordship on the stairs, the corpulent little Italian drew off his hat, revealing well-oiled black hair, and called, *"Buon giorno,* m'lord. For you, I hav'a found'a great treasure. One that's a gon'a make you *contentissimo*—very happy, *sì."*

William came down the stairs and waited as the energetic fellow, in his accented English, ordered his men to

enter. He bellowed at them to be careful of their cargo
when they bumped the door frame, then muttered a string
of what the viscount suspected were Italian curses.

The trunk was in fact an ancient leather-bound chest.
"This is all from one collection, *signore?*"

"*Sì,* the *barone,* he dies and his lady must'a sell to
cover his debts. He likes'a the old books, but he likes'a
the faro as well."

"What baron?" The viscount awaited the name with
bated breath as the bookseller's men were directed to the
library by the butler.

"Von Staub, m'lord. Hav'a you not'a hear of him?"

"Every notable book collector knows of Von Staub."
William's gaze was now riveted on the brass-studded
chest as the two lackeys who'd set it upon the table
moved back toward the library door.

"Then your'a interested in seeing what—"

"I'll purchase the entire chest," Borland interrupted in
a rush before the book dealer had shown him a single
item. Von Staub's collection was legendary. The baron
had begun as a young man in Austria, then he'd traveled
over much of Europe collecting first editions of noted
French, Flemish, and German poets, novelists, and theo-
logians.

Only Napoleon's arrival on the scene had forced the
gentleman to flee to England, where he'd continued to
add to his amazing collection. Rumor held that he owned
books that were the last surviving copies of certain
unique works.

Signor Fiorette's dark brows rose at William's impulsive offer. "You understand, m'lord, that many of these'a
books are in German and French dating back to the thir-
teenth century."

After receiving a nod from Lord Borland, the bookseller loosened the clasp and opened the trunk.

Seeing the numerous volumes, Borland's heart raced

with excitement as it never had for a woman. "As I said, I shall purchase the entire lot."

As the viscount stepped forward to inspect the literary treasures in Signor Fiorette's chest, a knock sounded on the library door and the butler entered, an outraged expression on his usually serene face. "There are two females outside, and one is demanding to see you, my lord."

William looked up with a frown. "We are not to be disturbed, Pinkney. I know of no female with whom I have business. Give them a small donation, then send them on their way." Dismissing the butler, the viscount turned back to lift one of the books lying atop the stacks in the trunk.

A female voice pierced the quiet of the book-lined chamber. "It ain't your money we're after, Lord Borland, but your time."

Dismayed, William drew the book to his chest even as he turned to see a female who looked slightly familiar brush past his butler, advancing on him with a martial light in her brown eyes. Short and sturdily built with red curls hanging from under a drab bonnet, she hadn't the look of a lady of Quality despite having a pleasing countenance. Behind her, lingering near the open door, stood a second female in a blue traveling gown, nervously tugging on a gold necklace around her neck. The viscount felt certain he'd never seen this one before, for he'd remember such a tall female.

Directing his attention back to the first woman, he impatiently snapped, "Who are you and what is your business here, madam?"

"I'm Nancy, my lord. Don't you rightly remember me? I'm one of Lady Margaret's maids and I've brung Miss Addington to you all the way from Basingstoke. She's just arrived from Rome to become a companion to her godmother, the countess. Her ladyship wants you to escort the young lady to Wother Castle in time for Christmas."

Fury settled deep within William's chest as his gaze moved back to the female in the doorway. Instinctively remembering his manners, he bowed. "Miss Addington, your servant." She was young and passably pretty from what he could tell under her unfashionable bonnet, but she had one remarkable feature, a pair of large pale brown eyes, thickly lashed, whose penetrating stare seemed to bare one's soul.

And his grandmother expected him to escort the lady to Scotland. William sighed with frustration. The countess was once again playing her matchmaking games. He'd made it perfectly clear he had no intentions of going to Kelso for Christmas, so she'd obviously done this to force his hand.

The young lady's engaging eyes grew wary even as she curtsied. "Lord Borland."

In that moment his ire was so great at the untenable situation, he turned once again to the maid. "Why did Lady Margaret not come for Miss Addington herself, Nancy? I am engaged in my own affairs here and haven't time to journey to Kelso this year, as I told my grandmother the last time we spoke."

Nancy's gaze veered guiltily away from the viscount's penetrating stare to survey the nervous bookseller. " 'Tis but two weeks until her ladyship's Christmas party, my lord. She has much to do in preparation and . . . well, you can't expect her to be jaunterin' cross-country and back at her age. Besides, you are here in London, so she thought you would gladly bring the young lady to her. 'Tis only another day and a half's drive from your estate."

The imperious old lady thought no such thing, and well he knew it. The old bird had played her hand and he'd not fall into her trap. "As I said, I have important business—"

"*Scusi,* m'lord," the book dealer interrupted. "If you're gon'a tak'a the lot, then our exchange is *finito* once we agree on a fair sum."

"Signor Fiorette, I want to know more about Von Staub's library. This cannot be the entire lot."

The Italian had no intention of telling the viscount that under the countess's orders he'd practically badgered Lady Staub into selling the few books in the chest. He merely shrugged, saying, "This'a was all the *baronessa* offered to sell."

The viscount paused at that intelligence, uncertain what to do as he looked from the bookseller to Miss Addington. He wanted the remains of Baron Von Staub's vast library, but was it for sale? And there stood Miss Addington, awaiting his help. There was a disconcerted or perhaps embarrassed expression on her face that told him she knew nothing of his grandmother's scheme to surprise him. Honor demanded that he take this young woman to his grandmother, yet the fact that he would have to fall in with Lady Margaret's little plot rankled him greatly.

To the viscount's amazement, the lady began to speak, but not to him.

"*Per favore, Signor Fiorette, potrebbe aiutarmi?*" Adriana directed her request to the bookseller. As an artist, she often saw subtle nuances in people's faces and she'd seen the angry glint in the viscount's blue eyes upon hearing who she was and what Lady Margaret wished of him. By his very words, Lord Borland made it clear that he knew nothing of her coming and had no intention of upsetting his own affairs to concern himself with a complete stranger. All she needed was the name of a place to stay until she and Nancy could arrange to take the stage north. After all, she didn't need his protection in the least. She always traveled with the small pistol her father had given her years ago.

"Ma parli Italiano, Signorina!" The stout signore's face lit with delight at having found someone who spoke his language like a native. With that the man offered his services in rapid Italian, and Adriana inquired about finding a posting inn as Lord Borland watched in baffled distraction. He read Latin, French, and German, but while he possessed a limited knowledge of Italian, he hadn't the least clue what was being said in the too-rapid flow of the pair before him.

Upon learning where one might board the northbound stagecoach, Adriana addressed the maid once again in English. "Nancy, 'tis clear Lord Borland is unable"—her tone expressed her doubts—"to accompany us to Lady Margaret's. We shall make our way to Holburn and engage seats on the York stagecoach."

With that the lady turned and made her way into the front hall. The maid and bookseller gave Lord Borland such dark looks, he felt like a veritable monster.

"Women are the most nonsensical creatures," the gentleman muttered out loud before he commandingly called, "Wait, Miss Addington!"

But to his annoyance, the lady didn't return to the library. Instead, she stood in the front hall, drawing on her gloves as if she were a grand duchess instead of a plain miss.

The viscount, still clutching the volume he'd yet to inspect, followed the stubborn woman out of the library so he wouldn't have to shout. "I haven't said I shan't take you to my grandmother. While it's true I have business at the moment, it seems it shall be rapidly completed. If you would care to wait in the drawing room with your maid, I shall make arrangements for us to leave this very afternoon."

"That won't be necessary, my lord. I do assure you I

am quite capable of going to Scotland without your assistance. Come, Nancy." Adriana's own ire had been raised by the gentleman's rudeness. She decided that Lady Margaret's grandson might be quite handsome with his sculpted face and tousled sandy-brown locks, but his lack of civility told her all she wanted to know. He was arrogant and rude, having little interest in anyone's concerns save his own.

The viscount's hand shot out and grabbed her arm. The blue of his eyes took on a steely glint. "Do allow me to escort you. Our English stagecoaches are not as safe as we might wish. In fact, I believe I must insist that you allow me to escort you."

Adriana's heart skipped a beat at the feel of his strong hand restraining her from leaving. There was something in his piercing gaze that said he would have his way. Nancy had informed Adriana on the coach ride to London that the gentleman was bookish. The image of a pale, bespectacled wretch afraid of his own shadow had formed, but nothing could be further from what Lord Borland appeared as he glared at her. Clearly he owned a fondness for books, but that didn't mean he was weak or malleable.

"A-as you wish, my lord."

The gentleman released his hold and without another glance at the lady ordered Pinkney to escort the guests to the Green Drawing Room. In what appeared to be an afterthought, he suggested refreshments for Miss Addington and Nancy while he concluded his business with Signor Fiorette. Saying that, he reentered the library without a backward glance, waited until Nancy exited, then closed the door on the women.

Adriana followed the butler to an elegant drawing room upstairs and pondered what to make of Lord Borland. He had been rude and domineering, but she told herself she'd not seen him at his best. What had Lady

Margaret been about to send her here without giving the man warning? There appeared to be some kind of long-standing dispute between grandmother and grandson. Whatever it was, she promised herself not to become involved. She would simply enjoy the luxury of traveling by private coach to her destination. Yet she couldn't deny that she would like the opportunity to sketch the viscount, for the strength in the angled planes of his face aroused her artistic interest.

Nearly two hours passed before Miss Addington and Nancy were summoned to the viscount's traveling coach, which stood in front of the town house. By that time, Adriana had become impatient, since she was nervous about meeting her godmother.

Settling into the old but well-appointed coach, she drew aside the green curtains to see his lordship personally directing his footmen to load two large trunks onto the coach. Afterward her own small portmanteau was put in, followed by Nancy's. His lordship then had a last word with Pinkney and the man who appeared to be his lordship's valet, vehemently protesting his being left in London. But Borland silenced his protest, saying something about Signor Fiorette calling with more information regarding Von Staub's library. After a farewell to the two older men, the viscount climbed into the carriage and they were off.

Already annoyed by her less than cordial meeting with Lord Borland, the length of time she'd been kept waiting for the gentleman to complete his preparations had only added to Adriana's pique. As the viscount settled opposite her, she couldn't resist venting some of her pent-up ire. "Two trunks? Had I any idea what a slave to fashion you are, I might have been better advised to go to Holburn after all, my lord. Nancy and I could have been nearly thirty miles closer to Scotland while you were choosing your wardrobe."

A crease appeared between the gentleman's brows. "Those are mostly books, Miss Addington, not my wardrobe."

Folding her gloved hands neatly in her lap, Adriana gave a look of disgust. "You mean we have been left to cool our heels while you decided whether to bring a copy of *Count St. Blancard: Or, the Prejudiced Judge* or *The Mysteries of Udolpho.*"

The look of outrage on the gentleman's face was ample reward for Adriana's barb.

"Miss Addington, I am a scholar. I have better things to do with my time than spend it reading cheap novels. In my opinion, Mr. William Lane should have been arrested for misusing paper with his Minerva Press. He would have been better advised to use the wood to warm his house than waste time and money turning it into paper on which to print that tripe. In truth, the fire is where those penny novels should be relegated. My trunk contains serious literature, science, and mathematics."

Adriana had never been a great reader of novels, but still, she couldn't resist pressing the point, if only to irritate this arrogant man from his superiority. "And have you read enough of Mr. Lane's books to fairly judge?"

"I would not waste my time in such a manner."

The lady exchanged a look with Nancy, who'd sat quietly during the exchange, thinking her mistress must be daft to have thought these two would suit.

"Well, I must say that seems unfair to the gentleman's business." Miss Addington then looked out the window as the carriage began to move.

Lord Borland crossed his arms over his broad chest. "I would have assumed at your age, Miss Addington, that you know life is rarely fair."

Adriana well knew the harsh realities of life. Having

to flee with her family from her home in Florence hadn't been fair, nor being separated from her brother at such a young age, nor the death of her parents. Harder still had been to leave her sister in Basingstoke and start a new life, but that was Adriana's fate.

She shot Lord Borland a defiant look, but he'd already pulled a small volume from his pocket and appeared to be reading, an annoyed expression on his face. It seemed to her that he was the one who knew little about life from the shelter of his title, wealth, and books. But she made no further comment, merely stared at the passing buildings and wondered how long it would take to reach Wother Castle, where she might part company from this disdainful man.

They traveled in uncomfortable silence. Soon Adriana's conscience began to bother her for her rude behavior. She had only herself to blame for not guarding her tongue. With a soft sigh, she made herself a promise to try to be more grateful for the trouble the gentleman was going through, no matter his disposition.

A great deal of traffic crowded the London streets, which hindered their progress. It took some two hours before they passed through Islington and gathered speed on the open road.

Lord Borland sat with a book in his hands, but in truth he read not a word. Instead, he tried to ignore this female that his grandmother had foisted upon him, but he found himself casting covert glances in her direction as she watched the passing scenery. She was nothing like the ladies who had pursued him so relentlessly during the Season in London or in the neighborhood near Borwood. She neither babbled inanities nor flirted. In fact, she appeared to have done her best to raise his ire over his habit of traveling with a small library.

He searched his memory for what he knew of the Addingtons. The girl's father had been a favorite of Lady

Margaret's, but as the third son of a baron, he'd set out to make his fortune on the continent and did not return before Napoleon shut down all ports to English shipping. There had been rare bits of communication over the years from which the countess had learned of his marriage and growing family. If William's memory was accurate, the countess had even helped the son when he'd arrived in Plymouth some years earlier. But there could be little doubt that she didn't know her newly arrived godchildren in the least.

It had been apparent to the viscount that his grandmother, upon learning the girl had returned to England, had hatched some grand plan to throw him and Miss Addington together. William almost laughed out loud as he realized that the countess would be surprised when she discovered that Miss Addington, far from being swept away on first meeting him, seemed to have taken him in dislike. A situation that suited him perfectly, he decided. But he truly couldn't blame her, for he'd been anything but polite and welcoming.

The viscount's carriage continued to move steadily north on the turnpike. Some thirty minutes later, their vehicle veered to the right, and a small gig could be seen to whiz past them on the left, carrying an older man and a beautiful young woman, who stared rudely into the Borland coach. Within a matter of minutes, Lord Borland realized their vehicle had begun to slow down.

The viscount reached up and slid open the communicating door on the roof. "What's wrong, Jock?"

The coachman called, "That fellow what passed us in such a rush is blockin' the road, my lord."

As his coach drew to a complete halt, William opened the door. The footman who rode on the back appeared immediately and lowered the stairs for his master. Borland had barely taken two steps away from the open door, when a large man with a round belly, dressed in a poorly tailored black coat, rumpled gray waistcoat, and round hat shouted, "I'm lookin' for Viscount Borland."

"I am Borland." His eyes narrowed. This fellow had the look of trouble, and he didn't need any more of that at the moment.

Seated in the coach, Adriana shivered, but she wasn't sure if it was the cold December air or the menace in the fat man's gaze as his bulging brown eyes locked on the viscount. She recognized the man as the driver of the gig. Behind him she could see the pretty blonde in a garish yellow gown stepping down from the small equipage, hurrying toward the two men. The young woman appeared to be in some distress as she dabbed at her eyes with a handkerchief.

The burly man belligerently barked, "So I've run ye to ground at last. Won't do ye no good to turn tail and run."

The young woman came to stand beside her traveling companion as he glared at Lord Borland. She began to tug on the man's dusty sleeve. "Papa . . . Papa . . ."

Lord Borland looked down his nose at his accuser. "Who are you, sir? And you had best have a good reason for this outrageous conduct."

"The name's Hunt, Barnabas Hunt, and one look at me daughter should remind ye of the reason." The man glared at his lordship as if he should know exactly who Mr. Hunt and his child might be.

The viscount gave Miss Hunt one brief glance. He saw a tearstained face that was pretty but would be beautiful when unblotched and smiling. She was dressed in a poorly cut round gown with too much green frogging upon the bodice and a high crown bonnet with a cluster of yellow plumes. Uncertain what Mr. Hunt expected him to see other than a female of questionable origins, he returned his angry gaze to the father. "Again I ask, why have you stopped my carriage in this manner?"

"Papa, Papa—" The young lady's voice grew more urgent.

"Hush, girl, I'll handle this."

"But, Papa, this ain't him." With that, the girl burst into sobs.

Mr. Hunt turned on his daughter, and taking her arms, he shook her. "Ye said it was Borland. Are ye lyin' bout that too?"

The girl shook her head, but with great gulps she said, "But . . . this ain't *my* . . . Lord Borland."

"As you can see, Hunt, I know nothing of your daughter, nor she of me. It appears she has been duped." But William felt a twinge of concern. Was there someone going about using his name?

Miss Hunt then fell to weeping with such earnestness that Adriana knew she must do something. She climbed down from the coach with the help of the footman, who still hovered near the door. Then without a word to Lord Borland she went straight to Miss Hunt, calling for Nancy to bring the wine from the basket the butler had placed in the coach. She led the girl some distance from the men to a toppled oak that had been pushed off the side of the roadway.

As they moved away, Adriana heard Mr. Hunt begin to question his lordship in a much more civil tone about being sure he'd never seen his Katy before.

"Come, Miss Hunt, sit here on this fallen tree."

It took some time to calm the distraught miss, but after several sips of the wine, she hiccuped out the information that her name was Katy Hunt and her father would turn her out if she didn't find her Lord Borland to take responsibility, for there was a babe on the way.

Adriana and Nancy exchanged a pitying look. Clearly, the girl had been seduced by some cad who had no intention of ever seeing her again, or why else the false name? Strangely, Adriana never for a moment thought the viscount was in any way connected with this lovely girl. She simply couldn't imagine the proud, bookish Borland stooping to ruining a female no matter how pretty or common.

"Are you certain your beau said he was Borland? You didn't mistake the name," Nancy asked, feeling sorry for the girl. The maid was well familiar with the lot of females of the lower orders when it came to dealings with the Quality. Too many babes came out the wrong side of the blanket with only the girl and the child suffering the blame.

Dabbing at her eyes, Katy nodded. "He were a lord, though he weren't exactly handsome. Came to Papa's inn for a week straight with his servant, a fellow with a great mole on his nose. The man told me on the sly that his master was Lord Borland." Then there was another great sniffle before she added, "His lordship said he loved me."

Nancy's gaze suddenly became more intense as it rested on the girl's face. "Was your lord tall with black hair low on his forehead, dark eyes, and rather longish arms?"

Katy looked at the maid, hope leaping into her slate-gray eyes. "Yes, do you know him?"

"Sounds like the viscount's heir, Mr. Randolph Jamison. But 'tis his man, Hickman, I recognize from the description of that great ugly mole on his beak."

On hearing the news that Lord Borland's cousin was involved in the girl's downfall, Adriana turned to stare at the gentleman still in heated conversation. The innkeeper seemed to be angrily saying something as he pointed at his daughter, and Lord Borland seemed to disagree as he shook his head. They could hear little of the conversation save his lordship's strong use of the word *no* each time Mr. Hunt spoke.

Adriana began to wonder if this arrogant lord was going to abandon Miss Hunt on the road when in fact his heir was very likely the culprit who'd ruined the girl. Coming to a sudden decision, she rose. "Nancy, take care of Miss Hunt. I must speak to Lord Borland immediately."

Without a thought about the consequences, Adriana marched straight to the gentlemen, who fell silent at her approach. She turned her dark gaze on the viscount and launched into a tirade. "My lord, you may never have seen Miss Hunt before this morning, but your family is very much responsible for her welfare. Nancy and I believe she was duped by your cousin. I insist that she be taken, if not to your estate, then to Lady Margaret's castle, where she can be properly cared for until after she has—" Adriana hesitated. She knew one didn't discuss such a matter. "Until her situation is resolved."

Even as she spoke, she could see Lord Borland's brows arch in outrage at her interfering in what he clearly saw as a matter that was none of her affair. "Miss Addington, pray return to the coach. I shall handle this delicate matter without your interference."

"I shall do no such thing until I have your assurance that something will be done for Miss Hunt."

His blue eyes blazed with anger, but before he could retort, Mr. Hunt spoke. "The matter of me daughter's been settled, miss. Lord Borland's done realized 'twas his heir what done the foul deed. 'E's to take the girl to 'is estate. But it does ease me mind to know that you'll be there to look out for me little Katy."

Adriana felt her cheeks warm. She'd assumed the worst about the viscount and had made a fool of herself by airing her views. "My lord, I am—"

The gentleman cut her off without a glance. "Will you now do as I ask and return to the coach, Miss Addington?" Not waiting for her response, he called to the maid. "Nancy, help Miss Hunt into the coach. She will be joining us at least until we stop at Borwood Abbey."

With that, Borland turned his back on Adriana and walked with Mr. Hunt to bid his daughter farewell.

Humiliated by her rash conduct, Adriana returned to the coach without comment. As she sat awaiting the others, the cold air failed to cool her flushed cheeks. It had been a reasonable mistake on her part. She'd seen little in Lord Borland that would lead her to believe he would give much thought to the troubles of others. She'd also heard him repeatedly answer no to something Katy's father was saying. It had all been very damning in Adriana's mind, but it appeared she was wrong.

She knew she owed the viscount an apology, but as the others climbed into the carriage, she decided she'd said enough for the time being. She would wait and seek the gentleman out after they stopped for the evening.

Avoiding eye contact with the viscount, Adriana noted that the footman appeared moonstruck by Miss Hunt as he helped the beautiful girl into the carriage. For her part, Katy seemed perfectly content to leave her father behind as she smiled coquettishly at the young man. A sudden thought flashed into Adriana's mind that the girl might be a hardened flirt and she would wreak havoc among the viscount's menservants unless a husband was found for her quickly. Adriana couldn't help but think it might do Lord Borland some good to have to pay closer attention to his surroundings.

The viscount climbed stiffly into the coach, not giving Miss Addington a glance. He inquired if Katy was comfortable, then being assured that she was fine, he again drew out the small book as the carriage began to move forward. The words on the page blurred as his mind wandered back to what had just occurred. His grandmother had rocks in her head if she thought he would ever consider a sharp-tongued female like Miss Addington to share his life. She'd actually thought he wouldn't do the proper thing by Miss Hunt. So, why did it bother him so much that she held such a low opinion of him? Hadn't that been just what he wanted?

He'd been held in contempt before by the young men at Oxford for his disinterest in cutting a dash about Town, but that had been because he had been different. This young woman seemed to find him lacking in basic decency and honor and that pricked his pride as nothing ever had.

After several miles, he decided not to give the lady's opinion too much worry. After all, he had only to deliver her to his grandmother, then he need never set eyes upon her again. With that, he tried to read, but the contempt in Miss Addington's amber gaze as she'd raged at him on the roadway kept coming to mind, and he was frustrated.

At last he looked across at Miss Addington and found himself staring straight into those same brown orbs, only now they looked contritely back at him before they looked away. With a sigh, he decided this was going to be a very long and trying trip.

Three

Nancy sat in a brown study as Lord Borland's carriage hurtled north at a steady speed. At the pace they were going since they'd cleared the London traffic, they would be in Kelso in scarcely three days' time. She was no fool. Lady Margaret wanted Lord Borland and Miss Addington to make a match of it, but between the pairs' seemingly constant disagreements and the speed of their travel, 'twas likely they would be in Scotland before the lady and gentleman had said more than three words to each other, and most like the words would be "Pray, drop dead."

Something must be done to slow them down. The maid knew she must come up with a plan. She pondered the notion of claiming she felt sick but then decided that wouldn't do. All her life she'd been amazingly healthy, and she looked it. Then her gaze settled on Katy Hunt. The girl's cheeks were very pale, and she appeared worn out as she slumped in her corner.

An idea flashed into Nancy's busy brain. The girl showed not the least signs of her condition in her high-waisted gown, but that didn't matter to Lady Margaret's maid. Katy would still be an excellent excuse.

"My lord, we must stop soon."

The viscount looked up from his book to stare at Nancy as if she'd just announced she intended to jump from the moving carriage. He frowned, then tugged out a watch and surveyed the time. " 'Tis only three o'clock. We have at least another two hours of light by which to travel."

"But we must think of Katy here, sir. She looks a bit out of curl with all this rockin' and rattlin' of the coach. Not that such a look is unusual for her delicate condition, but she needs to walk about a bit or she'll have no appetite for her supper. And we all know 'tis important for her to be properly fed."

The viscount pondered the maid's request even as he felt three pairs of piercing gazes awaiting his decision. He knew he would be found wanting in the minds of these females if he didn't make the proper decision. They were scarcely thirty miles from London, and this would make their third stop if one included the team changes. At this rate, it would take them a week to reach his grandmother's. But he wouldn't endanger Miss Hunt's health just because he wished to be rid of Miss Addington's company.

Without comment he opened the communicating door and ordered Jock to find a suitable posting inn to stop for the evening. Some twenty minutes later they pulled into a busy inn in the small town of Royston.

Within minutes of arriving, the ostlers at the Boar's Head immediately began to unload the luggage as Lord Borland escorted Miss Addington and the other women into the inn. The viscount quickly made their needs known to the innkeeper, then hesitated as he ordered a light tea to be served at five and for supper later. He didn't know precisely what to do about Miss Hunt. She was not a lady of Quality and in the normal course of things would not dine with him and Miss Addington. As he pondered what he should do, the young lady herself solved his problem, saying she was too tired to eat just yet and wished only a tray in her room later.

Nancy began to fuss over the girl, offering to take her

up to her chamber to help her settle. Her kindness had as much to do with helping Katy as it did leaving Miss Addington and Lord Borland in each other's company. She led the girl up the stairs behind a chambermaid.

William, hoping for some time alone and thinking Miss Addington would go to her room as well, turned to Thomas, his footman, a young man with shaggy blond hair surrounding a boyish face. The viscount never allowed his footmen to wear wigs after reading Dr. James Lind's treatise about cleanliness and preserving the health. "Where did the ostlers place my trunk of books?"

"I didn't let them gapeseed rascals touch yer books. *I* put them in the private parlor, like ye always want 'em, my lord." The footman gestured to a door down the hall.

Lord Borland turned to the young lady who lingered in the hall. "Until we dine, Miss Addington." With a bow he strode straight to a low-ceilinged room with raw beams and a roaring fire. He was looking forward to some time when he might read and relax. He opened the small trunk that sat on a table beside the windows and sorted through the books he'd brought with him.

He was debating over a very worn copy of Aphra Behn's novel of an enslaved African prince, *Oroonoko*, or a new purchase, Sir Charles Bell's *Anatomy of the Brain*, when Miss Addington's voice surprised him.

"My lord, may I have a word with you?"

Borland turned to discover the lady watching him as she stood warming herself by the fire. She'd removed her bonnet, displaying a cluster of neat black curls pulled to the crown of her head. She nervously tugged at the gold charm at her neck as she worried her full lower lip with even white teeth.

She really was a pretty chit despite being an inconvenience to him and having a rather sharp tongue. There was a hint of impatience in his tone. "Yes, what is it?"

"I want to apologize for my conduct on the road. I

had no right to impugn your honor in that way." The young lady tilted her chin upward slightly as she added, "I can defend myself only by saying that all I could hear of your conversation with Mr. Hunt was you repeatedly saying no to the man, which led me to believe that you intended to abandon Katy."

The viscount eyed Miss Addington thoughtfully. He felt certain this trip was going to be far longer than he'd planned, and to be constantly at dagger-drawing with the young lady would only make the journey seem that much longer. In truth, he'd allowed his anger to make him behave less than gentlemanly to the chit on their first meeting. It wasn't her fault that his grandmother had hatched this scheme of them traveling together.

"Miss Addington, what you overheard was me trying to convince Mr. Hunt that I wouldn't abandon his daughter at some inn after he was gone. That I wouldn't turn her out after she delivered her child, nor would I force her to send the babe to some foundling home."

The young lady's amazing brown eyes seemed to glitter with emotion. "Oh, you make me ashamed. I did truly think wrongly of you, sir. Pray, say you will forgive me."

The viscount frowned, his gaze dropping to the book still in his hand. "If you will forgive my rude reception of you at Portman Square. I fear I took my ill temper at my grandmother out on you. Perhaps the countess is right, that I spend so much time with my books, I quite forget how to conduct myself properly."

The young lady laughed, a deep, husky sound that William found surprisingly enticing.

"I do not blame you, my lord. I cannot imagine what Lady Margaret was thinking to have not warned you of my coming. But we have now smoothed out our differences and shall continue our journey in harmony."

To Borland's surprise, she came forward with her arm

extended as if they were agreeing to a pact. He was amazed at how small and soft her hand felt in his. He shook it quickly and then moved past her to the fireplace as a strange desire to trace his fingers over her lovely face filled him.

Behind him she said, "I see I am disturbing your peace and you will soon be wishing me gone again. I think I shall take a walk about this lovely village."

The viscount looked over his shoulder as she made for the door. "Be certain that you take either your maid or Thomas. 'Tis not the thing for a young female to be out without a servant."

Miss Addington grinned at him as she put her hand upon the door handle. "I am quite familiar with the way things are done in England. My aunt spent the entire week reminding us of the rules that govern a young lady's conduct. Besides, my father was forever telling us tales of his youth. In truth, young ladies here have much more freedom than the females of Italy. It has often made me glad that my father was English. I look forward to living the life of an Englishwoman."

He eyed her a moment, then gave a half-smile. "Then you won't object that I have asked for tea at five o'clock?"

"I shall be prompt, my lord."

With that, the young lady left the viscount to the peace and quiet of the private parlor. He settled in front of the fire, but the book lay unopened on his lap. He suddenly wondered what life must have been like for Miss Addington, growing up in a foreign land. He knew relatively little about her, yet she exhibited practically no discontent for her circumstances. He would almost say she held a zest for experiencing life, both the good and bad. He realized he knew someone else like her, his grandmother.

Maybe fate wasn't so whimsical. His grandmother and Miss Addington would be far better suited than he and the outspoken young lady. With a decisive nod of his head, he opened the book and began to read about the human brain and all its infinite mysteries.

The clock on the mantelpiece chimed five times as a knock sounded on the door of the private parlor. The viscount looked up, surprised to find himself in some-place other than his library. He called for the visitor to enter.

Thomas opened the door, and one of the inn's maids hurried in with a tray laden with sliced meats, cheeses, bread, and small poppyseed cakes, as well as a pot of tea. "My lord, your tea is ready."

"Summon Miss Addington, Thomas."

"I done looked for the lady and her maid, my lord. They ain't in the inn nor on the road out front."

William frowned as he glanced at the clock. She'd left for a walk over an hour before. What might have happened to delay her? It would be dark soon and the temperature would plummet. "Come, we must search for her."

Grabbing his hat and greatcoat, William exited the inn, crossing the yard to the main street. With Thomas beside him, the viscount looked up and down the busy road, but there was no sign of Miss Addington or her sturdy maid. Anger began to build in him. He hated when people weren't punctual, and why did it always seem that women were the worst offenders? She'd promised to be back on time. A bitingly cold wind brushed his cheeks, and he knew there was no time to delay. "You look in that direction and I shall go toward the north."

The viscount walked rapidly down the main street of Royston, stopping occasionally to peer in shopwindows or look down the side alleys. The young lady or her maid were nowhere to be seen. His anger was soon replaced by growing concern. Something might have happened to the pair. Then, as he neared the end of town, the sounds of a female voice raised in anger reached his ears.

He veered down a side street, following the sound. He could hear Miss Addington's voice clearly but not the words. She angrily berated someone in rapid Italian. Rounding the final corner, William discovered himself in a large open courtyard in front of an ancient warehouse. Miss Addington appeared to be in a tug-of-war with a brawny man who had a great deal of dust and dirt coating his person, from his gray beard and hair, down his leather apron, to the worn work boots he wore.

The object of the dispute was an urchin who was even more filthy than the man. His employer tried to pull him from Miss Addington's determined grasp. With each tug, Nancy flailed the gentleman with her reticule, but to no avail.

The young lady's gaze lit on Lord Borland. "My lord, you must help at once. This beast is abusing the boy frightfully."

At that, the man gave a great tug on the boy's grimy coat and nearly pulled Adriana to the ground. The lady staggered, then righted herself before she once again drew the lad back toward her.

"Ye can't take me brick boy. It ain't legal. I done paid his da fer him. He's learnin' the trade."

"All he is learning is that you are a cruel monster, sir. Lord Borland, this man struck the child with that stick."

Borland's heart dropped. What had Miss Addington gotten herself into now? It appeared to be a dispute with some fellow over his apprentice.

His gaze dropped to the child in question. The boy looked to be about eight, but it was hard to tell beneath the grime. "Why were you striking the child?"

The brick maker straightened at the sound of the gentleman's voice but didn't release his grip on the lad's clothing as he cast a belligerent gaze on his lordship. "He's clumsy, m' lord. Done broke two bricks today when we was loadin' the wagon."

Miss Addington shook her fist at the man. *"Santo cielo."* She briefly rolled her eyes toward the heavens, as if looking for the very saint she'd called upon. " 'Tis no wonder. He is too small to be carrying such great bricks about. You must let the boy go."

The viscount glanced at a crumbled brick lying beside the partially loaded wagon. It did appear quite large, measuring eighteen inches or more, but he knew the brick maker was within his rights to punish the boy for its loss. "Miss Addington, the lad is learning a trade. He is—"

Dark eyes flashing, she turned on Lord Borland. "You cannot be so heartless to leave him with this beast. I have seen your kindness to Miss Hunt. Can we not help this lad as well? Surely you could find a position for him on your estate."

"I weren't abusin' the lad. Just cuffed him on his head, m'lord. Ye can't be takin' me rightful property."

The viscount decided it would be pointless to explain to the impassioned young lady that there were thousands of these young children throughout England who were sold into apprenticeships each year. It provided the children with a way to learn a trade. One simply couldn't demand their release. About to refuse her request, his gaze locked with the boy's, and there was such entreaty in the child's green eyes, Borland knew he couldn't abandon the lad to the brutal brick maker.

"What's your name, boy?"

"Nick, m'lord."

"Has this man been beating you?"

When the brick maker tried to protest his innocence, Nancy hissed him to silence. The lad shot a frightened look at the glowering man, then met the viscount's eyes once more. With the wisdom of one far older, the lad knew better than to rely on a gent involving himself in such affairs, so he offered a tactful reply that wouldn't incur future reprisal should this group lose interest in his plight. "Well, I do be frightful careless. These 'ere bricks is 'eavy."

His lordship's eyes narrowed when the brick maker yanked the boy from Miss Addington's grasp.

"See, I telled you how it was."

The boy cringed, and a resigned expression settled on his small features.

William reached for his money, reading between the lines. With a determined glint in his blue eyes, he asked, "What will you take for the boy?"

At first the man would accept no offer, but as the viscount increased the sum, the brick maker began to have such a look of avarice in his eyes that one knew Lord Borland was paying far too much. At last money changed hands and the lad was released to Miss Addington. Nancy stepped forward and began to fuss over the boy as if he were her own.

After the brick maker departed, happily counting his money, and Nancy and Nick had started down the alley toward the main road, the viscount put out a hand to restrain Adrianna. "I appreciate that you have a kind heart, but many of these children would starve if they weren't taken to learn a trade. You must realize you cannot save every forlorn creature in England, Miss Addington."

"I do, Lord Borland. I can save only the ones who cross our path." With a defiant toss of her head, she followed after Nancy and the boy.

Borland raised his eyes to heaven, hoping God would grant him patience. He stood for a moment in the growing darkness, wondering why it was Miss Addington couldn't be like other young ladies, totally absorbed in her own affairs to the exclusion of all else. But in truth he knew that were he not the one suffering the results of her kindness to others, he would admire her selflessness.

He suddenly realized that at the rate they were increasing their passengers, his carriage was likely to look like the York stage by the time they reached his estate, a collection of grubby urchins and down-on-their-luck females crowding the roof. He would have to convince Miss Addington they'd picked up their last stray, unless she wanted to ride up on the box with Jock.

Having stopped to find an ostler to go in search of Thomas, Lord Borland stood in the hall of the Boar's Head, removing his greatcoat and hat, when a bloodcurdling yell echoed from the private parlor he'd reserved for their use. With a sigh, William wondered what new disaster was in progress.

Upon entering the room, the viscount discovered Nick standing on a settle against the wall, holding Miss Addington and Nancy at bay with a straight-back chair. The lad's cheeks were puffed out like a squirrel who'd just stumbled on a store of nuts for the winter. Clearly, he'd helped himself to their untouched tea still on the table.

"What is the meaning of this commotion?"

Nick's mouth was so full, only garbled sounds came out. Then he began to chew in earnest as Adriana began to explain. "He doesn't want us to give him a bath. He thinks washing his hands and face is sufficient for his needs."

The viscount felt a sudden urge to shout just like Nick. Since the arrival of this young lady in his library, it had been one thing after another. But he schooled his features to remain placid. "You will take a bath, young man, or you will not travel with us to Borwood Abbey in the morning."

After a great gulp, Nick looked at the remaining food. "I'm like to catch me death of cold. Can't I stay and 'ave another bite or so, m'lord?"

"You may have your fill . . . *after* you are clean." The gentleman's tone brooked no argument.

Conflicting emotions played on the young boy's face as he stared at the tray of food. At last his desire for such a sumptuous repast overcame his fear of a fatal illness brought on by water. He stepped down from the settle, putting the chair back on the floor.

Nancy, all business, came to put her hand on his thin shoulder. "Come, my fine lad, I shall scrub you from top to bottom, for certain I am you've not had a good cleanin' in years."

Nick's green eyes grew round as he drew back. "Wait a minute! I done said I'd take a bath, m'lord, but ain't no female gonna be a-washin' me."

Hands on her hips, Nancy bristled. "I wouldn't trust you to give yourself more than a lick and a promise with a bar of soap, my filthy little scamp."

Nick's face set into mulish lines. "Ain't no female givin' me no bath, not even for an entire roast pig nor all of a cake."

The viscount glanced at Miss Addington, and her mouth twitched as she resisted the urge to smile. "Then you will just have to wait until his lordship's footman returns, for there is no one else to supervise you. The innkeeper's servants are too busy with the other guests."

Nick looked from Nancy, who tapped her foot impatiently, back to the food waiting on the table. But his modesty won out. Folding his arms across his thin chest, he sat down on the settle. "Reckon I'll just 'ave to wait while you 'as your cat lap till this 'ere footman comes."

Borland knew by the expression on Miss Addington's

face that she would not sit down and eat in front of the hungry boy. The viscount was also certain the young scamp was counting on the lady's soft heart. He came to a quick decision.

"Come with me, Nick. I shall see you properly cleaned so that Miss Addington can have her meal in peace."

Nancy's eyes grew round. "You'll wash the lad, my lord?"

Despite the inconvenience, the viscount smiled at the shocked servant. "I am quite capable of supervising one small boy's wash. I shall make certain he scrubs every inch, Nancy."

While the viscount went to arrange for a hip bath and hot water to be sent to his room, Nick dashed to the table and stuffed several slices of ham into his mouth. Nancy could have stopped him, but she didn't have the heart. All she did was warn him.

"You take my advice, my fine scamp, you'll do just as his lordship tells you without a word of protest. If you're to work for Quality, you can't be lookin' like some dustbin."

Nick nodded his head as he happily stuffed a slice of roast beef into his bulging mouth. At that moment Lord Borland returned, calling to the lad to follow him.

As the door closed behind them, Nancy shook her head. "I never thought I'd see the day when Lord Borland would put down a book long enough to be actin' the servant for the likes of some ignorant, filthy lad."

Adriana sat down at the table, eyeing what young Nick had left. "I think you all have underestimated the gentleman. He has a kind heart along with his thirst for knowledge." With that, she requested Nancy bring a fresh pot of tea, for the first had grown quite cold and she found herself as sharp set as young Nick had been.

Upstairs, the viscount waited beside the roaring fire in his chamber until the inn's servants finished filling the metal hip bath with warm water. Then, as they left the room, he looked at Nick. "Shed all of those clothes, for I am certain you are sharing them with a variety of unpleasant creatures that I don't wish to add as our traveling companions."

"But they're me old friends."

The viscount needed only to cock one brow.

Nick looked unhappy, but he remembered Nancy's warning and did as bid, stripping off his coat and shirt without complaint. As he bent to pull off his shoes, the viscount's face grew grim. "Did the brick maker put those stripes across your back?"

The boy shook his head. "Not all, m'lord. Me da done some of them when I was slow doin' what 'e said. But I've learned me lesson. I'll be good at whatever ye want me to do, I swear."

The viscount suddenly felt ashamed, not of the privileged life he'd led, but for how little thought he'd given to the fate of those who were born into poverty. He'd been angry at Miss Addington for interfering in matters he felt didn't concern her, but if not for her, this boy's life would have been one of continued abuse.

Still, Borland reminded himself that not all men who took apprentices were brutal employers like the brick maker. The truth was one couldn't go about taking every young lad away from such positions or the streets would be filled with fledgling pickpockets.

As Nick splashed into the water, the viscount went to the table and picked up the soap the innkeeper's wife had provided. "Make certain you wash your hair, behind those ears, and the back of your neck."

The boy took the soap and sniffed. "I'm gonna smell like a female."

"Better that than a rubbish pile, my boy."

The boy grinned. "That's just what your pretty wife said, too, on the way back 'ere."

The words jarred Borland. "The lady is not my wife but my grandmother's companion." He suddenly had an image of what life with Miss Addington would be like, forever involved in some dispute or another while the lady tried to save the world. It didn't bear thinking about.

Lathering his hair, Nick couldn't see his lordship's face as he added, "Well, if I were a gent right and proper, I'd marry the lady. Prettier than any mort I ever seen, and nice too. I like all them foreign words she spouts."

Just then Thomas arrived, saving the viscount from making a comment. He allowed Nick to explain his rescue and saw the startled look that settled on the footman's face to hear of his employer's involvement. Thomas knew his lordship wasn't unkind, merely oblivious of what went on beyond the pages of his current book.

While the boy chattered, the viscount realized Nick had spoken the truth. Miss Addington, besides being pretty, had a genuine good heart. It didn't make him suddenly want to disrupt his life to fall in with his grandmother's plans, but he could at least admire her good qualities.

When Nick finished his tale, the viscount gave his footman instructions to find clean clothes for the boy before they set out the next day. He suggested the innkeeper might be able to provide the boy with something to wear that evening.

Leaving the lad in his servant's capable hands, the viscount went downstairs. Entering the private parlor, he saw Miss Addington still seated at the table, the remnants of her tea before her. She rose, a smile lighting her face. The viscount was surprised at the strange sensation that took place in his gut.

"Do come and have your tea, my lord. I must apologize for having gotten you involved with this matter. I was certain Nancy and I could handle that brute, but alas, it was not to be. I can only say thank you for your kindness."

Uncomfortable with her praise, considering he hadn't wanted to involve himself in the beginning, the gentleman merely said, "We have a full carriage now, Miss Addington. Will you promise me not to go looking for any more strays?"

Eyes wide with innocence, the lady replied, "I didn't seek out either Miss Hunt or Nick. But in all honesty, my lord, I am glad that they found us, for we were able to help them. Don't you think the unexpected makes life far more interesting? Now I shall go see how Katy fares, for I am certain she must be quite frightened being away from her home for the first time."

The viscount watched as the lady exited the room. He rang for a tankard of ale and a new tray of food, since Nick would soon be down and ravenous. As William awaited the arrival of the tray, he thought about what Miss Addington had said and frowned. All unexpected events did was disrupt one's life, and that was the truth.

Four

To Lord Borland's vexation, the morning was well advanced by the time his party was ready to depart the following day. First Nick had managed to disappear for nearly an hour, which required Thomas make a search for him. When the footman returned empty-handed, Lord Borland began to suspect that the lad might never be found. Then, sometime after breakfast, the boy, clean blond hair gleaming in the winter sunlight, appeared, looking quite proud in his new clothes as he trudged up the main street of Royston, a small bundle of his meager possessions nestled under his arm. He informed his lordship he'd been home to tell his ma of his good fortune and bid her farewell.

At last, when everyone prepared to board the coach, Katy experienced a severe bout of morning sickness. After some dry toast and tea, the innkeeper's daughter pronounced herself fit to travel. The viscount, concerned about the young woman, decided they would stop every few hours to allow her to rest. Upon hearing this, Adriana hurried to the boot of the carriage and begged Thomas to find her portmanteau. She opened her bag to retrieve her sketchbooks and pencils.

As the carriage pulled out of the yard of the Boar's Head, Nancy eyed the items clutched in Adriana's lap. "What have you there, miss?"

"I am hoping to do some sketching of the countryside

while Katy recovers herself at the stops." She smiled at the young girl, who still looked a bit pale.

"You're an artist? Her ladyship will be monstrous pleased. She adores painters and is forever buyin' some new fellow's work from a London gallery."

Adriana cast a nervous glance toward Borland and laughed. "Dear me, Nancy, Raphael was an artist, Michelangelo was an artist, Botticelli was an artist. I, on the other hand, draw pictures to amuse myself."

Nancy's curious gaze locked on the sketchbook. "Have you any pictures in your book we might see?"

Adriana hesitated a moment. Her family had always praised her work, but she'd long suspected they were much prejudiced by their love of her. She'd also been able to sell the small sketches she'd done of the piazzas to the locals in Rome to keep her and Amy from starving. But somehow she didn't feel as confident having her work under the scrutiny of Lord Borland, a sophisticated gentleman who'd likely seen all the finest masters in England.

Glancing across the aisle, she realized he had closed his book and was paying a great deal of attention to their conversation. Despite her fear of having her work disparaged, she opened the older of her sketchbooks, giving it to Nancy.

"Oh, Miss Addington, I don't know about them other fellows you mentioned, but I think this is beautiful. Don't you, my lord?" With that, the maid turned the sketchbook around and showed William Adriana's drawing.

Borland, prepared to make some polite remark, was struck speechless by the beauty of the woman with the sad eyes in the portrait. "Who is she, Miss Addington?"

"My mother, but the sketch isn't very good, for I was scarcely fifteen at the time I drew it. Unfortunately, she died soon after, so I never got a chance to try another sitting."

The viscount reached out and took the book from Nancy. He marveled at the work. The young lady owned a talent with a pencil, for one could see how she'd captured more than just an image. The very soul of the woman seemed to speak from the picture. There was sadness and pain etched in the lady's lovely face that only a true artist could capture without rendering the subject an object of pity. He looked at Miss Addington with a new respect. He knew he wanted to see more.

"Do you mind?" he asked, half lifting the page, indicating he would like to peruse the contents of the sketchbook.

Adriana clasped her hands together nervously but nodded her permission for the gentleman to view her work.

A series of family portraits covered the first portion of the book. Miss Addington identified each as the viscount flipped through. Her grandfather the *conte* looked stern but regal in his library in Florence, her own father gentle and smiling as he sat under a tree in Tuscany. Next came a picture she'd sketched of her brother and sister near a waterfall, talking. Nancy commented on their resemblance to Adriana.

Then came a series of images of the local residents of Rome—a baker, a flower vender, a mother and child beside the Tiber River. Nancy oohed and ahhed over the work, but the viscount said little.

At last Lord Borland stopped at a picture that seemed to affect him deeply. "This is the Colosseum, is it not?"

"It is, but I fear my meager skills cannot do it justice."

With awe in his voice, the viscount stared at the drawing for a long time, then handed the book back to Nancy. "That building is magnificent."

The maid eyed the sketch with doubt. "Well, miss, I'm sure you've done a wonderful job, but it looks like a giant pile of stones and crumbled walls to me."

Adriana smiled as she remembered young Amy had

thought the same. "It is a great ruin, Nancy, a remarkable feat of architecture built in the first century A.D."

The viscount nodded his head. "Started in seventy-two A.D. and dedicated in eighty A.D. by Titus."

Nancy sniffed as if that weren't so long ago. "Well, miss, I'm sure we got finer ruins right here in England for you to draw. Why, some old Roman had 'em build a wall here in England from one coast to the other up near the border. We'll pass right by it on the way to Kelso."

The viscount smiled at Adriana, making her feel a strange fluttering in her chest. "She is referring to Hadrian's Wall, but I fear it isn't worthy of your obvious skills. All that remains is little more than a big stone wall and a series of very crude forts. It wasn't the Romans' finest effort."

Adriana felt a warm rush of pleasure race through her at his praise of her work. Feeling flustered by his unexpected flattery, and in an effort to gather her wits, she took back the book. She forced her mind to concentrate on that picture in her sketchbook and not Lord Borland. "Nancy, the Colosseum's not just an ordinary ruin. You cannot imagine its true size unless you stand beside it. When it was in use, they could seat nearly fifty thousand spectators." Her eyes sparkled at the memory of the huge structure she'd drawn so long ago.

"Fifty thousand! What would they be wantin' to put that many poor souls in a single building for?" Nancy frowned.

Adriana loved nothing better than talking about Rome. "It was an amphitheater. The Romans held contests to the death between great warriors they called gladiators, or between gladiator and animals. Why, they would even sometimes have mock naval engagements staged in it."

The maid's face grew doubtful as she stared at the

sketch. "Naval battles? Don't see how. Wouldn't the water pour out all those holes?"

Adriana and the viscount laughed. Borland again took the sketchbook from Adriana, then pointed at a spot. "They didn't fill the entire amphitheater, just this one section here at the bottom. I have read it was very impressive."

Seeing that Lady Margaret's maid was entirely unimpressed, the gentleman, who had been amazed with Miss Addington's knowledge of the subject, asked, "What book did you read to learn so much about the Colosseum, Miss Addington?"

Adriana's delicate brows arched upward. "Book? I didn't read about it, my lord. As I sat drawing the structure, an old man who came there every day told me a great many things about its history. That was the old way information was passed down from father to son and still is in the poorer sections where they cannot afford books. In truth, I was sad to finish my picture, for I found the old gentleman's stories very interesting."

His lordship seemed surprised, but the lady had piqued his interest. She'd genuinely seemed to understand the region's history. "What other legendary areas of interest did you see?"

Taking back her sketchbook, Adriana smiled. She could talk for hours about Rome. She and Alexander used to sneak out before dark and play in some of the ruins. Just talking about that beautiful city made her dear brother seem closer. "My lord, Roma is one great history lesson. Nearly every corner you go around you see some legacy from the old Roman Empire."

The viscount enjoyed the way she said the word *Roma* with such feeling. It suddenly made all the facts seem more interesting to hear the town called by its Italian name. Soon the pair fell into a discussion of all the ancient areas in Italy that Adriana had visited and what she knew of the country's history.

Nancy had little interest in the details about a lot of old ruins in a foreign land that the lady and gentleman discussed, but she sat with a smile on her face as if she were listening. For the first time since they'd set out on their journey, Miss Addington and Lord Borland were enjoying each other's company. It gave the maid hope that Lady Margaret's wish might yet come true.

Progress north proved slow that day. As promised, the viscount ordered his coachman to stop within a few hours at some small, out-of-the-way inn for Miss Hunt's health. To Nancy's disappointment, the viscount moved off to sequester himself in a private parlor, intending to have only a book as his companion. Young Nick had other ideas. To the maid's amusement, the lad trailed after the gentleman, pestering him with questions about how much farther and what he'd do once they reached his lordship's estate.

After seeing Katy was resting comfortably, Nancy joined Miss Addington and they walked about in the cold morning air. The young lady sketched a thatched cottage as the maid watched in awe.

Still, all was uneventful, and within an hour everyone was back in the carriage, ready to journey north again. His lordship looked a bit frazzled by his new devotee and seemed to enjoy a reprieve from the lad's chattering. As the coach exited the inn yard, Katy tried to convince the viscount that another stop wouldn't be necessary that day. Since she'd eaten a light nuncheon she felt more the thing, she declared, but the viscount insisted she mustn't overdo.

In truth, when the next two-hour interval passed, the young girl welcomed the chance to rest, finding herself surprisingly fatigued. As Nancy helped Katy up to her room, Adriana stood in the cold afternoon sunshine, scanning the horizon for some point of interest she might draw. All she could see were vast expanses of fallow fields and trees.

Nick suddenly appeared at her side. " 'Is lordship says I'm to stay with ye, miss."

Adriana stifled a smile, knowing Borland had likely never read a word at the last stop with the boy in the same room. "I should be delighted to have you join my walk."

Eager to be on her way, she halted a passing ostler and asked if there was anything of interest nearby that she might use as a subject for a drawing. He directed her to a path just beyond the inn that he declared would lead her back to the river they'd crossed to reach the inn. At the end of the trail she'd find a crumbled church that was thought to be quite beautiful.

About to depart, Adriana's heart lurched when suddenly Lord Borland exited the inn. He stopped and looked around, his face a study in exasperation. Then his gaze lit on her and he came toward them.

"May I join you and Nick for your stroll, Miss Addington? The landlord's only private parlor is engaged, and I wouldn't be able to read a word in that busy public room."

She wasn't sure why, but Adriana experienced a twinge of disappointment that boredom and not a chance to share her company had driven him to join their walk. "We should be delighted, my lord. But I must warn you that we have been told there is little of note in the neighborhood save a picturesque old ruin of a church beside the river."

Lord Borland gestured her forward. "Lead the way. I need a bit of exercise. This trip is turning into quite the journey."

Adriana glanced briefly at Borland, puzzled by her strange reaction to him. She'd been surprised at how much she'd enjoyed their discussion in the carriage that morning. He'd reminded her of an eager child wanting to know all about the things she'd seen during her years in Italy. She decided once one got to know William, he really wasn't so stuffy.

The pair walked in silence down a small dogcart trail that took them to the river. Nick ran ahead, stopping occasionally to beckon them onward or to pick up a stick and toss it into the woods.

Lord Borland suddenly interrupted Adriana's thoughts. "Do you miss Rome, Miss Addington?"

"A bit, but in truth I miss my family more. If there is one thing I have learned, my lord, it's that one can be happy anywhere as long as you know your loved ones are safe and happy. We didn't wish to leave my grandfather's villa in *Firenze*, but for our own safety we had to go. Yet, despite the obvious restrictions, we were happy in *Roma*."

"Restrictions?"

Adriana smiled. "Papa always feared we might forget and speak English in public and would be found by the French, so unless he accompanied us, we were rarely allowed out of the courtyard behind the *pensione*. In truth, there was more danger for us in his badly accented Italian than in our speaking English."

The viscount laughed. "My French tutor always decried my accent, but your English is perfect, not a hint that you didn't grow up in this country."

"Thank you. I have Papa to thank for that. He hired an English nurse away from one of the families traveling through Italy when Alexander was born. He felt it important that even the distant heir to a barony must speak properly, even though it's likely my brother shall never inherit. If I behave with decorum, I have dear Nurse to thank, for she insisted my sister and I always comport ourselves like proper English ladies. She lived out her final days with us in *Roma.*"

Just then they rounded a small outcropping of rocks and came upon the remains of the old church. Nick came running up. "Are ye goin' to draw that old pile of stones, miss?"

Adriana breathed a sigh as she took in the picturesque beauty. The building sat at the edge of the river, framed by two old oak trees. Time had preyed heavily upon the structure and little remained but what would have been the main sanctuary. She softly breathed, *"Bellissima."*

The viscount eyed the destroyed building with interest. "I would guess it to be early seventh- or eighth-century architecture." As he moved closer to inspect the ruin, he suddenly stopped. "I don't want to be in your way if you wish to sketch it."

With a sad shake of her head, Adriana moved past Lord Borland. " 'Tis very lovely, but the intricacy of the small stones in the building would require more time than we have at the moment." She looked around. "Instead, I shall sketch the river, for it reminds me greatly of the one we visited every Sunday morning."

Borland looked a question. "You went to a river every Sunday just outside *Roma?"*

Adriana nodded. "We were masquerading as an ordinary Italian family, but we couldn't attend Mass at the local cathedral, having been baptized in the Church of England. So, each Sunday we would tell the landlord we were going to a cathedral across town. Then we would travel out of *Roma* and spend the day beside a lovely little river. Now I shall leave you to explore the church while I go draw the river and the bridge I see through the trees. Come, Nick, we'll allow his lordship to inspect the ruins in peace."

The lure of the ancient church beckoned, but the viscount couldn't put aside thoughts of how difficult the young lady's life had been. Imagine growing up under the constant threat of being discovered and thrown into prison! Not for the first time did he believe that his own life seemed utterly dull with its lack of turmoil. He truly admired her, having been through all that, yet she didn't appear to be the least bit bitter. Like the piece of smooth marble he spotted in the rubble, he realized that Miss Addington had survived her family's difficulties unmarred.

Adriana glanced over her shoulder with a smile as the viscount stopped to inspect closely an engraved marker. He seemed to have a truly insatiable thirst for knowledge. When he looked toward her, she waved, then followed Nick, who dashed in front of her.

"Nick, be careful," she called when the lad rushed about at the river's edge, nearly falling in as he slipped on a stepping stone. With a shout of joy, he jumped back and forth from the water-smoothed rocks to the bank, all the while shouting, "Look at me, miss."

With the idea of keeping the noisy boy from interrupting Lord Borland's tour of the ruins, she pointed out a path that ran east along the riverbank. "Shall we go a bit closer to that lovely old bridge?"

Nick, too delighted with his good fortune of being out of the brick maker's employ, readily agreed and skipped along the path. The boy chattered incessantly, quite unused to having anyone pay the least attention to him.

At last Adriana found a position halfway between the bridge and the ruins. Nick immediately suggested they go inspect the old stone overpass, but she announced she intended to render a drawing of it instead and would he join her. Reluctantly, the lad settled beside her on the rock she'd chosen and watched as she started her drawing.

Several minutes passed, and the picture on paper was

beginning to take shape. Suddenly the clip-clop of a horse could be heard. In minutes a rider on a great lumbering animal came into view from behind the trees. He looked like a farmer with his rough-hewn clothes and battered round hat, and his horse appeared more accustomed to pulling a plow than taking a fence. The man crossed to the center of the bridge and stopped. As the pair beside the river watched, he untied a sack that seemed to be alive and moving, then hurled it into the water. Without a word, the fellow turned his shaggy horse around and trotted away.

"Did you see that, miss? That fellow done tossed somethin' in the river."

Adriana's gaze had never left the sack from the moment it left the farmer's hand. The discarded pouch moved swiftly toward them on the fast-flowing current. Something pushed frantically against the sides of the oilcloth. Had someone rid themselves of an inconvenience? A cat or dog? The bag jerked and sank lower in the water. Whatever was inside, it was still alive. Action was her only choice, or the bag's occupant would drown.

"Nick, find me a long limb." She dropped her pencil and sketchbook, never losing sight of the still-moving oilskin bag.

As the boy searched for a branch in the woods, Adriana moved toward the sinking bag that still floated downstream. Mournful cries emanated from the slowly sinking pouch sounding very much like a cat. "Hurry, Nick."

The boy quickly returned with a long, thick limb. She ordered him to stay on the bank. Using the stones that protruded from the water at irregular angles, she made her way almost to the middle of the river. After several tries she snagged the bag with the limb and pulled it carefully toward her. She feared any moment the branch would break and the bag, now saturated, would be drawn beneath the surface.

It took several attempts, but at last she grabbed the drawstrings on the bag and lifted it, dripping, from the water. The resident inside yowled dreadfully, poor, frightened creature. She tossed the limb into the water, then turned to make her way back to the bank. To her surprise, she discovered Lord Borland had joined young Nick on the riverbank.

"Miss Addington, are you trying to kill yourself?" His face was set in stern lines. "Have a care. Should you fall in out there you would be pulled under in a moment with all your heavy clothing."

"Have no fear, my lord. Despite being a mere female, I am quite agile."

The man and boy watched as she worked her way back across the stepping stones to where they stood. As she neared the bank, she wavered slightly on an uneven stone. Borland angrily called, "Do be careful, Miss Addington. The water is now shallow, but you will catch your death of cold should you become wet this time of year. My grandmother would think I had tried to do you in deliberately."

Upon reaching the bank, the viscount took the oilskin sack from Adriana, helping her make the final step to dry land safely. She was amazed at the feel of strength in him with that simple gesture.

Without further comment, he knelt to untie the drawstrings as she and Nick gathered around. The head of a very large smoke-gray cat with golden eyes, fur wet and matted, peeked nervously out of the opening.

"Oh, the poor thing." Adriana reached down and lifted the soaking wet animal, drawing it to her woolen cape. "I have always adored cats."

"Have a care, Miss Addington. The animal will soak your clothing, and it may be vicious, or, worse, diseased. That would account for the man trying to destroy it."

"It looks perfectly healthy to me. What a dreadful

thing to do, throwing it in the river. The poor little thing is shaking from the cold."

Nick eyed the animal's bulging belly. "Ain't so little if ye ask me. Reckon she's about to 'ave kittens, miss. Just too many mouths to feed for the farmer."

The viscount looked at the boy in surprise. At the tender age of eight the child already knew the harsh facts of his world. Looking back at Miss Addington cuddling the frightened feline, William felt a growing disquiet as she fussed over the dripping cat. Hoping to put a stop to any thoughts of keeping the animal, he remarked, "There is no need to worry so about the creature. We shall make certain she has a good home at the inn. No doubt we can give it to the innkeeper's wife and that efficient woman will see to its needs."

Adriana's face took on a beseeching expression. "I know you said we couldn't take any more strays with us, my lord. But surely this poor creature cannot take up such a great deal of room. I promise I shall take care of her myself, and she won't disturb you in the least." She gently stroked the cat's head and added softly, "I've never had a pet of my very own."

With a sigh, Borland realized he was finding it more difficult with each passing hour to resist the lady's pleading eyes that looked amber in the daylight. The more he got to know her, the more he realized how much she'd missed in her strictly protected life under French domination.

Still, he needed to exercise some controls, for the lady was like the Pied Piper, drawing more and more unfortunates along with her. At least her motives weren't as sinister as the fictional piper's, but that didn't make his coach any less crowded. Yet, as he watched her stroke the cat, he realized he couldn't refuse such a simple request.

"Very well, but don't be disappointed if your new pet

disappears suddenly before we reach Kelso. I cannot think the animal will greatly enjoy traveling by carriage with strangers."

At the mention of Scotland, Adriana frowned. "Do you think Lady Margaret would object to my having a cat?"

Remembering the much-doted-upon Boris, the Russian hound, Borland knew the last thing the countess would want in the castle was a cat about to produce a litter of kittens. Then he was struck by the justice of this situation. With a wolfish grin, he replied, "How could the lady be anything but enthralled?"

As they made their way back to the inn, the young lady and Nick discussed what they should name the cat. Only half listening, the viscount reveled in the irony. He couldn't wait to see his grandmother's reaction to her new companion's pet. It was about time the countess got a taste of her own medicine, and what better way than to have her life disrupted as she was forever disrupting his?

The December sky grew ominously gray as the travelers continued north that afternoon. Their newest traveling companion had been relegated to a small crate atop the vehicle, to Nick's delight. For the remainder of their day's journey there were no further interruptions to their travels, but as they neared their destination in the fading light, gusts of wind from an impending storm began to rock the well-sprung carriage. Just after five o'clock his lordship's party was welcomed at the posting inn, the Royal Arms, in Grantham, where he always stopped on his rare journeys to London.

By six Adriana, having quickly washed and changed, sat in the rear parlor, listening to the wind whistle around the inn. A maid busily set the table for their supper as Nick lay in front of the fireplace, playing with the cat, who appeared content with her new lot in life. The lad had decided that since the animal was to be Miss Addington's, and the lady being newly arrived from Italy, she must give it a name in one of those foreign words like she'd shouted at the brick maker. So to please the child, Adriana had dubbed the cat Signora.

She watched Nick dangle a bit of red ribbon before the playful feline. Looking up at the clock, Adriana wondered what was keeping his lordship. She hoped nothing was amiss, for she was certain that in his view this trip had been just one annoyance after another. Suddenly, she realized her thoughts were beginning to dwell too much on the viscount, and she decided that wasn't safe. He was very handsome but far too set in his staid ways. To Adriana, it seemed as if he had no desire to know people except as characters in books. Yet, as they'd talked in the carriage, his desire to hear of all she'd seen was like a thirsty man seeking water.

Still he was no callow youth. He appeared well content with his studious life and clearly wasn't interested in effecting any changes. And a wife would certainly be a change for such a singularly solitary man. Nancy had hinted as much. The fact that his grandmother had gone to such lengths to bring the two of them together in this odd manner told Adriana that the lady was convinced her grandson would not marry without a push. If there was one thing Adriana was certain of, it was that she didn't want a reluctant groom. And so she would inform the countess if the lady continued her matchmaking once they reached Wother Castle.

Her thoughts then turned to the lady who was to be her employer. Would she like Lady Margaret? Everything she'd heard about the lady made her seem, if not eccentric, at least an original. It might prove to be an interesting post. Certainly, the countess sounded nothing like her grandson.

A knock on the parlor door interrupted Adriana's musing. The innkeeper's wife, a plump, rosy-cheeked woman, entered the room, shooing out the dawdling maid. "Ah, Miss Addington, I brought your pet a bowl of cream and the lad a tart since he's already had his supper with the coachman."

"Thank you, Mrs. Watley. I'm sure they will greatly enjoy such treats, but you must be quite busy and shouldn't inconvenience yourself on our account."

The woman placed the bowl on the floor for the animal and handed Nick a plate. The boy grabbed the apple tart and began to devour it with a delighted glow in his green eyes.

"Why, miss, 'tis my pleasure. Lord Borland's been stoppin' here as long as I can remember, and right pleased we are to at last see him takin' a young lady up to meet his grandmama, for we've had the pleasure of serving her ladyship as well."

Adriana felt her cheeks warm. "Oh, you mistake the matter, Mrs. Watley. The viscount is merely escorting me to Lady Margaret's. I am to be her new companion. I am not . . . that is . . . we are not betrothed." For the first time, Adriana felt some sympathy for the viscount's situation. It seemed as if everyone of his acquaintance was in a conspiracy to find him a wife.

A look of genuine disappointment settled on the woman's plump face. "Well, if you'd pardon my sayin' so, miss, you couldn't find a nicer gentleman to wed than the likes of Lord Borland, and I know what I'm talkin' about, for we have all kinds stayin' here."

The woman moved to the table and began to straighten the utensils the maid had placed by the plates. Then she observed more to herself than to Miss Addington, " 'Tis unfortunate that young ladies always overlook the quiet ones. But to my way of thinking, they are less likely to be leavin' one in the lurch when you need 'em the most."

Stung by the remark, Adriana felt the need to defend herself. "I haven't overlooked his lordship, I assure you. I have reason to know he has many fine qualities. He will likely make the right sort of lady a wonderful husband, should he decide to marry. But I don't think I'm that lady, Mrs. Watley. Our temperaments would never suit." After Adriana made the comment, she suddenly felt strangely low, but she didn't have time to dwell on the reason.

At that moment the door to the parlor opened and Lord Borland entered. He'd changed into a dark blue coat over a pale gray waistcoat and looked very handsome with his sandy-brown hair arranged à la Brutus. He arched one brow when he saw his grandmother's companion and the innkeeper's wife in conversation, then politely asked, "Is our supper ready, Mrs. Watley?"

"I was just awaitin' your arrival, my lord. I'll have Sadie serve at once. Come, Nick, and leave his lordship and Miss Addington to have their dinner in peace."

As the door closed behind the departing pair, Borland moved to the fireplace. "I must apologize for keeping you waiting, but traveling without my valet leaves me feeling like I have two left hands sometimes."

Adriana looked up at him but didn't smile at his little witticism. "I have a bone to pick with you, my lord."

The gentleman looked a question.

"I understand from Nancy that Lady Margaret still has that great hairy dog my brother wrote me about and won't likely welcome our Signora in the least."

The hint of a wicked smile tipped the gentleman's sculpted lips, making Adriana's heart skip a beat. She suspected deep down in that well-mannered, scholarly exterior there lurked a true pirate, only the gentleman didn't realize it as yet.

He drew his hands behind his back before he replied. "But do you not see how someone the countess has continually bedeviled would leap at the chance to give her back a little of what she's dispensed so freely? Likely she won't welcome anything that would upset her beloved Boris. I realize it was a foolish lapse in good manners, but the fact remains that my grandmother is forever interfering in my life. For one brief moment I reveled in what she would do if I were to pay her back in kind, but of course I shan't. We shall give the animal a home at the abbey."

Adriana smiled. She didn't tell him, but she found she liked him better knowing that he had a bit of playfulness mixed in with his staid and bookish nature. "I am certain that Signora will make an excellent mouser wherever she lives."

His lordship gazed at the flames, making no comment for the moment. A thoughtful expression settled on his face, then with a sigh he said, "You don't know the countess, Miss Addington, but I'm sure you will soon learn that I am a great disappointment to her. She would have preferred a grandson who drank hard, rode hard, played hard, and seduced every barque of frailty who might wish it. A dashing rake or a famous Corinthian would have been her choice. A notorious buck who after some minor bit of scandal broth finally found some equally dashing female to tame him. Lady Margaret's great fear is that I shall end my days alone and, even worse to her thinking, unmarried."

Surprised by the sudden confidence and fearful that the gentleman was becoming too melancholy, Adriana said, "Or that you will go dotty in your old age and marry the abbey's tweeny, as some lords have been known to do. Is yours very pretty?"

The gentleman's incensed gaze darted to Adriana's face, but seeing the twinkling brown eyes watching him, his own features relaxed into a smile. "I don't even know if I employ a between stairs maid, Miss Addington. But knowing my grandmother, that is just what she is thinking."

At that moment the maid arrived with bowls of turtle soup to begin their meal. The pair took their seats and enjoyed a fine dinner of only four removes. They conversed easily on a variety of subjects. Adriana found William's reading had left him well informed on nearly every topic, and he found her to have a surprisingly sharp mind, a fact that didn't entirely take him by surprise after having spent several days in her company.

After the covers had been removed and they'd finished the apple tarts and cheese, Adriana rose to bid the gentleman good night.

"Before you go, Miss Addington." The viscount went to the chest of books that Thomas had put in the parlor. He rummaged around for a moment, then held up a great leather-bound tome. "Since you have spent most of your life in Rome, I thought you might like to borrow my copy of *The Decline and Fall of the Roman Empire*. It would fill in many of the details about the ruins you saw every day but didn't know what they were."

Adriana eyed the book warily. The sheer size of the volume he held was daunting. But she didn't want to appear ungrateful to him for his kindness. "You are very generous, sir. But I hope I won't offend you by telling you I am not a great reader. In fact, I have a series of books in my case that my aunt gave me before I left Basingstoke and I haven't even opened one yet."

William was surprised at the disappointment that raced through him. She'd been so knowledgeable of the historical details of the Colosseum he'd been convinced that she'd want to know more about Rome. But he understood that that wasn't the case. Seeing the uncertainty in her eyes, he realized he'd made her uncomfortable. "I am not offended in the least. It isn't important. I know everyone doesn't own my fondness for reading, and it was just a thought. Pray, have a good night's rest, Miss Addington. Hopefully, if the severe weather holds off, we should reach the abbey by tomorrow night."

With that, the young lady curtsied and said good night. The viscount took the book he'd chosen for Miss Addington and made his way over to the fireplace, where Signora lay curled on the rug, asleep. He sat in the chair Adriana had occupied earlier but stared into the fire, puzzled at his reaction to the lady's refusing his offer of a book. Why should he care if his grandmother's companion didn't like to read? It wasn't as if the countess had ever had a companion reading sonnets to her.

Then his mind veered to the way the candlelight had reflected blue-black lights in her dark ringlets. And the white arch of her lovely neck as she'd turned her head each time the maid had brought a new course. He remembered the sparkle of the gold charm nestled into the valley of the soft mounds showing above the lace ruffle of her bodice. Suddenly realizing where his thoughts were leading, he abruptly rose. He couldn't be attracted to Miss Addington. He would never give a second glance to a woman who didn't share his interest in books and learning. Why, the very notion was unthinkable. On that determined thought he took himself off to bed.

Five

The following afternoon, snow swirled about Lord Borland's northbound carriage as it rumbled along the nearly obscured road. The storm had held off until noon, then tiny flakes began to fall, but it intensified with frightening speed. William watched the deepening blanket of snow on the frozen ground and knew that his desire to reach Borwood Abbey that night might well be thwarted by the weather. Within the last hour the flakes had increased to such an extent that visibility had dropped to only a few yards. He sighed with frustration, for he'd been looking forward to the comfortable familiarity of his library.

While the other females in the coach showed concern about their safety in the face of the seeming blizzard, Miss Addington could only marvel at the beauty of the snowflakes. She delighted in the increasing storm, asking how deep the viscount thought the snow might become.

Seeing the frightened look in Miss Hunt's eyes, he only said, " 'Tis hard to say. One can never be certain about how long the snowfall will last."

But Katy was very frightened. "Oh, miss, you can't know how dangerous travelin' in such a storm might be. Why, the coachman could run us in a ditch and we'd freeze afore we could find safety."

The viscount shook his head. "That is hardly likely on such a well-traveled road as this. Besides, my new coachman is an excellent driver. That is why I hired him."

Katy tugged her cape tighter and stared out at the growing storm. "I do hate bein' cold."

Thinking to take the chit's mind off the weather, the viscount looked for a topic. His gaze lit on the gold charm he noted Miss Addington always wore. She had an unconscious habit of moving it back and forth on its chain, especially when she was nervous or distracted, but at the moment it lay at rest against her blue traveling gown. He could tell it had something etched on the front, but from where he sat it was unclear.

"May I inquire about your pendant, Miss Addington? The inscribed picture seems unusual."

Her fingers flew to her treasured keepsake, and she smiled. " 'Twas a gift from my brother before he left *Roma*. The etching is of the warrior goddess Minerva. Alexander hoped the medallion would give me wisdom and prudence, both of which he clearly thought I lacked at the time he presented the gift. He declared with such virtues I might find my heart's desire."

Thinking that an advantageous marriage would be the usual desire of a female, the viscount was curious what this unusual young lady's heart's desire was. "And what would that be, Miss Addington?"

"I haven't exactly settled on whether I would be most happy traveling about to new places, for I greatly enjoyed my voyage to England, or joining my brother after he returns from France. Following the drum should prove exciting."

Before his lordship could comment, the communicating door atop the coach slid open. A shower of snowflakes fluttered in before young Nick's face appeared in the opening. "Jock thinks we must stop at the next inn, m'lord. The snow is so fierce, 'tis like drivin' with our 'eads two foot up a snowman's arse."

A choked laugh was stifled from one of the women, but when the viscount looked at Miss Addington, all he could detect was that mischievous twinkle in the depths of innocent amber eyes.

Jock's muffled voice could be heard chiding the lad for his loose tongue in front of the women. With a quick apology, the lad waited until his lordship gave his order for the coachman to use his best judgment, then closed the door.

Within minutes the coach pulled into the inn yard of a small posting house called the Grey Dove. It was an ancient timbered building with mullioned windows, clearly without many available rooms by the number of carriages outside. The inn looked as if it had seen better days, but at the moment it was a welcome sight to the cold travelers. Assisted from the carriage, Adriana hurried through the snow, and the others quickly followed. They found themselves in a small public room with three long tables, but despite the building's age, the room was clean and the furniture well polished. Due to the storm's intensity, several groups of travelers had already taken refuge and were seated at the tables.

Upon inquiry, the viscount discovered the innkeeper had only two private parlors, and one had been previously engaged by Mrs. Arthur Biggles and her two daughters, who were traveling to their estate in Carlisle for Christmas. The owner of the inn, seeing the gentleman's frown, became very apologetic, saying they rarely had Quality stop, but what with the storm he presently had little space and the ladies would have to share a room. Adriana assured the viscount that she had no objections.

As Lord Borland ordered meals for his party, Adriana and Nick, who'd retrieved Signora from her crate before climbing down from the box, followed the viscount's footman into the rear parlor while Nancy and Katy were led upstairs. Adriana inspected the chamber as Thomas set the viscount's trunk of books on a table near the windows. The room proved to be small and dark, but the roaring fire was welcomed after the cold morning in the carriage. Adriana drifted to the small mullioned windows, attempting to peer out, but the ancient glass was too distorted to see anything but gray light.

The footman looked around, his face showing that his employer was used to far better accommodations. " 'Tis a pity about there bein' only the one small parlor since there's so much time to kill but looks like his lordship won't be able to do no readin' here."

Surprised, Adriana asked, "Why is that, Thomas? All he might need are some candles and the gentleman can read to his heart's content."

"Wouldn't be proper for him to read with you to entertain, miss." Then Thomas lowered his voice as he nodded his head at the boy who leaned dangerously close to the fire, warming his hands as Signora rubbed against his legs. "Then there's that young scamp, Nick. He's a bit of a prattler, miss. His lordship ain't exactly decided what the lad's goin' to be doin' once we arrive home, so he's a bit underfoot here, since Jock and I have duties and can't be watchin' him. You can't be trustin' the child to a sorry lot like ostlers or he's like to learn some bad tricks."

Realizing they had the entire afternoon to idle away in the inn and possibly even longer if the storm proved severe, Adriana decided that it would be to all their benefit if the viscount got a bit of peace and quiet. "Never fear, Thomas. I shall make certain Lord Borland has a parlor to himself, at least for a couple of hours."

The footman smiled, then bowed. "Very good, miss. Will that be all?"

"Would you discover if the innkeeper has a wife and send her to me?"

Thomas bowed and left the room. Within minutes a

rather harried woman with smudges of flour on her angular face arrived, carrying a handful of tallow candles and a pewter candelabrum. Several minutes' conversation elicited the information that Mrs. Daniels had three children. After lighting the candles, the innkeeper's wife took Nick off to meet one Dickon Daniels in the kitchen with orders not to return for several hours.

The viscount stepped into the room just as the pair were departing. "Where is the lad off to?"

"Mrs. Daniels is taking him to the kitchen to play with her son. I didn't think you'd mind, since he doesn't have any duties."

"Mind having a bit of quiet? I think not." With that, the gentleman moved to the fire. "And how would you like to while away this long afternoon, Miss Addington? I fear the weather shall keep you from your usual occupation of walking and drawing. Shall I have the landlord search out some cards for us? A game of piquet perhaps?"

The gentleman's lack of enthusiasm for the suggested card game made Adriana laugh. "I could also spend the afternoon pulling out your fingernails, which, no doubt, you would derive equal pleasure from."

The viscount laughed. "Was I that obvious?"

"You were, sir, but have no fear, I have been seated in a carriage far too long to wish to be seated playing cards. I believe I shall go up to my room and rest, like Miss Hunt."

His intense blue eyes searched her face. "That truly isn't necessary, Miss Addington. You are welcome to stay here. I won't force you to play cards."

Adriana moved to the door. "If you don't mind, I really do want to rest a bit, and should I become restless, who knows, I might even become desperate and try one of the books that my aunt gave me."

William smiled as she closed the door. He suspected

she'd arranged for him to have some time alone. It was a kind gesture considering he hadn't been the most enthusiastic host. His gaze traveled to the trunk full of books awaiting his pleasure. Knowing this might be his last period of peaceful reading until after he delivered Miss Addington to his grandmother, he quickly retrieved the book he'd been reading about Rome, then moved a chair near the fire.

He had scarcely begun the first page when, to his surprise, Signora jumped into his lap, turned around in a circle, then settled down as if she'd always done such. He stared at the animal a moment, then hesitantly stroked the cat's head. The feline began to purr contentedly. It was strange. All his life he'd avoided small animals, but there was something quite pleasant about running one's hand over the fur. It was as if some connection were made by that simple act.

Being careful not to disturb the now sleeping animal, William reopened his book with a contented sigh and began to read.

Nearly two hours later the parlor door opened and Thomas entered carrying a tankard of ale as well as slices of apple, cheese, and bread. He moved a table close to his lordship, then set the tray down without making a comment. He lit several more candles, then moved back to the door. Just as the oaken portal was about to close, the footman heard the viscount's "Thank you, Thomas." But the gentleman's gaze never lifted from perusing the book.

Deep into the history of Roman emperors, William paused when a thump sounded on the far wall sometime later. Thinking it must be the Biggles ladies in the other parlor, he went back to his reading, but after a moment the sound came again. Only this time it was two thumps, one right after the other. With a glance in the direction of the noise, the viscount realized it had come from the outer wall and not the adjoining room.

Then a thought occurred to him. Thomas had come to the viscount's employ after he'd rescued him from a bout of fisticuffs at an inn in Northumberland when Borland had been on his way to visit his grandmother for her birthday the past February. The lad had filched a loaf of bread from the innkeeper's wife and had been set upon by the burly ostlers of the Merry Monk. William saved the young thief that day, but Thomas now owned an intense dislike of ostlers. There had been several incidences since then during the viscount's rare trips to York, but the footman promised to mind his manners after the last dustup.

William hoped the footman wasn't in any trouble. He waited a moment, listening, but all was quiet. With a slight shrug, he returned to his book. Just as he turned the page, there were four or five more thumps against the wall. Worried it might be Thomas and a bit annoyed at having his reading disturbed, the viscount put his book on the mantel, lifted Signora to the floor, and went to open the window.

He lifted the latch and pushed open the window. In that second a giant ball of snow splatted in his face. Opening his eyes, the viscount discovered Miss Addington, Nancy, Nick, and a young lad he assumed was the innkeeper's son staring back at him, a look of horror on all their faces.

Wringing her hands, Adriana called, "Don't blame the others, my lord. I was the one who convinced them to come out to build a snowman, but it turned into a snowball fight. 'Tis my first time of playing in the snow."

"Don't move, Miss Addington," the viscount barked, then disappeared from the window.

Dickon escaped into the rear of the inn as Nick moved

to where Adriana stood in the snow-covered field behind the inn. "I reckon we're in for it now, miss."

She suspected he was right. "Don't worry. I won't let you be turned off before you've even had a chance to begin, my boy."

By the time the viscount, trailed by his footman, reached the rear yard of the inn, both Nick and Nancy had moved to flanking positions beside Adriana, as if they intended to protect her from the gentleman's wrath. The viscount stopped just as he came around the corner and eyed the trio with an expression on his face that none could read. Was he merely annoyed, or truly angry?

To everyone's amazement, William, Lord Borland, gentleman and scholar, suddenly bent down and scooped up a handful of snow. With a shouted "Let them have it, Thomas!" the gentleman hurled his snowball. The game footman grabbed for his own icy weapon and sent it flying through the air. The women and child had been at the game for a while, and all quickly dodged the missiles.

With a great deal of laughter, the air was soon full of snowballs flying in all directions even as more fluffy flakes drifted down from the sky. Each time someone made a direct hit, there came a moan at the feel of cold, wet snow. The victim always came back with a barrage of snowballs at the thrower. The members of his lordship's party dashed about in the waning storm, oblivious of the cold and their growing dampness, until a particular large missile thrown by his lordship at Nick missed and landed squarely in Adriana's face. The unexpectedness of the blast caused the young lady to lose her footing and fall into a small snowbank.

Hurrying toward her, the viscount asked, "Are you unharmed, Miss Addington?"

Stretched out in the snowdrift, Adriana suddenly thought that Lord Borland looked like a Roman god as he stood towering over her, his hand out to help her up. She decided the cold must be affecting her brain. She gave Borland her hand and laughed. "I am fine, my lord. It is, after all, only water."

As the viscount easily pulled her to her feet, he frowned. "My dear Miss Addington, your hands are like ice." Chafing her cold-reddened hands between his larger ones, he looked at her blue traveling gown showing under her woolen cape, taking note of the wet spots where she'd been hit. "I think it time we put an end to this game, else you are likely to catch your death of cold."

Adriana wondered how he could think her hand felt cold when his very touch had suddenly made her warm all over. She told herself it was merely caused by the vigorous exercise. But when she drew her hand free, their eyes locked for a moment and she felt breathless.

From behind them Nick shouted, "The snow's stoppin'."

With an effort, Adriana broke her gaze from those mesmerizing blue eyes. She noted that the flakes no longer fell in the growing darkness. Attempting to sound utterly normal despite the rapid beat of her heart, she said, "Well, sir, I suppose we must put an end to the fun. It seems our ammunition has ceased to fall."

The viscount laughed but made no comment. He merely followed Adriana as she made her way back to the inn. As she hurried up to the room with Nancy trailing behind, Adriana wondered if Lord Borland had experienced the same sensation at that moment in the snow. What could she be thinking? The two of them were like opposite sides of a coin, and it would be best if she remembered that.

Human behavior was a complete mystery, Lord Borland thought as he stood in front of the fireplace, staring at the flames while awaiting Miss Addington for supper. What had come over him that afternoon? He'd gone out to read the riot act to the lot of them and instead had joined in their childish game.

But deep inside he knew what had caused his unorthodox behavior. The three of them had stood staring at him as though he were a three-headed ogre, and he'd hated that feeling. He'd remembered how he'd felt that year at university when so many of the young men called him Lord Boring behind his back. His friend Jonas had told him about the nickname, thinking he would find it a great joke. Instead, William felt ostracized and wanted to return to the safety of Borwood Abbey at once. But he hadn't; he stayed for the whole miserable year to prove something to himself, if nothing else. He was capable of bearing adversity on his own.

For some strange reason, he didn't want Miss Addington to think of him in that same derogatory manner. Why he should care what some female thought was beyond him, but he hadn't uttered a word of reprimand. Instead, with the snow falling all around, he'd flashed on another incident from his childhood. He'd been barely ten years old, staying at an inn with his mother. They'd been on their way to London to see a doctor about his mother's persistent cough. He'd seen several boys playing in the snow and wanted to join in the fun, but his mother had adamantly refused, calling it childish nonsense and citing the danger to his health.

This afternoon in the inn yard he suddenly wanted his day in the snow. A smile touched his mouth as he thought about having done something so utterly out of character. His friend Jonas or even his neighbor, Perry, had they seen William, would have thought he'd lost his mind. But the game and Miss Addington had been quite amusing.

A knock sounded on the door, and Miss Addington

entered looking lovely in a simple white merino gown trimmed in dark ruched blue ribbon. "I do hope I haven't kept you waiting, my lord."

He gestured for her to take the seat by the fire. "Not at all. But tell me, have you suffered any ill effect from being so wet and cold?"

Adriana smiled as she arranged her skirts after sitting. "I have not. I do want to thank you for being so understanding this afternoon after catching a snowball on your face. I cannot deny 'twas I who hurled it. I fear my aim is rather dreadful."

Somehow learning she was the culprit didn't surprise William, and he said, "Then I believe we are even and you cannot complain about my mishap of hitting you." He smiled down at her, liking the way the firelight played upon her face.

"Of course, there is a difference. Having lived in England all your life, you are an experienced snowball thrower, whereas I am a novice," she teased.

"As to that, I have never thrown a snowball in my life until today."

Adriana's brows rose in surprise. How could he have never played in the snow having grown up where it snowed every winter? But she made no comment, only wondered about his strange upbringing that had made him so serious. "Well, as for my complaining about such a mishap, I believe most men think complaining is supposed to be a female's prerogative. My father always asked my sister and me the rhetorical question 'If a man is standing in the woods alone and he speaks, yet no woman hears him, is he still wrong?' " The lady smiled up at him, those amber eyes twinkling.

William threw back his head and laughed heartily. "A truism if ever I heard one. I do believe I should have liked your father very much."

Adriana's gaze dropped to the flames. "He was a remarkable man in his own way. I think it took a great deal of courage to defy his father's wishes for him to take holy orders and set out for the continent with only his wits to live on. Yet I think his one regret was that it left him estranged from everyone in his family save his sister, my aunt Vivian." She fell silent, lost in memories of the sadness on her father's face whenever he spoke of his brothers.

The viscount suddenly wondered how his life might have been different if he had been full of defiance at his own mother's smothering attention. Yet he knew his mother had had an advantage over most. She'd wielded her ill health as a powerful weapon whenever he'd strained against her control. And why should he think of that now? Was he not satisfied with his life? His gaze returned to Miss Addington, looking lovely but bemused. As his gaze locked on her full rosy lips, he wondered how sweet they would be to taste. Disturbed at the direction of his thoughts, he moved restlessly away from the fireplace to the window. "I think we should be able to reach Borwood Abbey on the morrow if the roads are passable. 'Tis a good sign that the snow has stopped so early."

Before Adriana could comment, a maid arrived with their supper. They enjoyed a companionable meal despite the poor quality of the food. After Miss Addington bid the viscount good night, he looked at his box of books but decided he wasn't in the mood to read. Instead, he settled in front of the fire and contemplated his life.

As the logs shifted and crumbled to glowing embers, William knew that the young lady his grandmother had foisted on him had made him reconsider his solitary existence. It wasn't that he suddenly didn't enjoy learning new things, but why had it always been in the armchair in his library? But he knew why—first there had been his mother, then habit.

There was so much of the world that he hadn't seen. Perhaps he should bring Randolph to the estate and turn over the responsibilities of the day-to-day operations to the fellow, giving himself the opportunity to travel. Then he remembered Katy and his cousin's suspected role in the girl's downfall. How could he bring his heir to the abbey if Randolph was as truly debauched as William now suspected?

Suddenly rising, he cursed his grandmother's interference in his life. He'd been perfectly satisfied before she'd sent Miss Addington to him. He decided that he would be perfectly happy with his life once he got the disturbing young lady off his hands. On that note, he went to his books and made a selection, then sat down, trying to put his discontent from his mind.

Six

"How much farther to the abbey, my lord?" Nancy asked, peering out the carriage window at the light fog that seemed to have sprung up as they entered a forest of snow-coated evergreens. The towering trees blocked out much of the gray light, making it dark and gloomy in the carriage, which moved at a slow, steady pace. That morning the roads hadn't been impassable, but as the day progressed the surface once again began freezing solid. The coachman continued onward but the progress was slow.

His lordship narrowed his eyes while he tried to determine the landscape through the mists. " 'Tis difficult to tell exactly, but I think we are but a few miles—"

A gun fired from the woods nearby. Katy threw up her hands and screamed, then a voice outside shouted, "Stand and deliver!"

The carriage halted abruptly, and the same voice could be heard calling for the coachman to throw down his barker. Within seconds a man in a black cape, his face obscured with a mask and a round hat, appeared at the door, a pistol in his hand. Other shadowy figures could be seen moving in the fog behind him. He yanked open the door. "Why, look'e what we got here. I'd thank ye kindly to step down, me pretties, and ye too, m'lord."

The highwayman used the barrel of the gun to flip down the stairs, then he offered Adriana his hand with a gallantry at odds with his role. But she refused. Grabbing the carriage door to steady herself, she descended, her knees shaking. Within a matter of minutes, all the interior passengers stood on the roadway. Katy whimpered as Nancy stood with her arms around the girl. Adriana knew it was foolish, but she felt strangely safe standing beside Lord Borland. Thomas hovered at the rear of the carriage while Jock and Nick watched from the box, helpless.

The viscount reached into his pocket and pulled out his purse, tossing it to the villain. "Take this and leave the women alone. They are servants and likely to have less funds than you."

The statement startled Adriana. He thought of her as a mere servant. But then, that was what a companion was, wasn't it? Merely an upper servant. Her gaze returned to the pistol the brigand waved, and she thought her status hardly mattered at this exact moment. Looking up, she stared into the man's hazel eyes, which seemed to radiate evil, and she froze.

The thief grabbed the pouch, but his gaze shifted to the women. "Servants, ye say. Looks like ye's setting up a harem, m'lord, for they're a right pretty lot. Still, I'm wantin' to see their hands for any rings they might be hidin' and maybe take a peek in them little bags on their wrist." He pointed with his pistol at the reticules that dangled from the women's arms.

He started with Katy, whose hands shook as she extended them to show she wore no jewelry, then he quickly rummaged through her handbag, finding a few coins. When he was done he reached up to tweak her cheek. "Can I have a kiss, me pretty?"

"Let her be. Take the money and be gone." His lordship took a menacing step forward, but the highwayman again leveled his gun at the viscount. Adriana could see

Lord Borland's jaw clench in anger, but he stood as he was ordered, having little choice in the matter.

The brigand turned back to Katy, but before he could claim a token of affection, Nancy shoved her bag in front of him. "Cease your yammerin', fool, and be done with it. 'Tis too cold for your nonsense. If you intend robbin' us, do it and don't jaw us to death."

The hazel-eyed thief merely winked at Katy, then searched Nancy's bag and took her few quid. He moved on to Adriana, who clutched her bag beneath her cape, hoping he wouldn't take it. He grinned at her and said, "Another pretty one?" but then his gaze shifted lower and the evil glint seemed to glow in his eyes.

"What have we here?"

He reached out to take the gold necklace. Adriana's hand instinctively flew to her neck to stop his effort.

"No, please, 'tis all I have from my brother."

She tried in vain to cover her treasured good luck charm, but he roughly grasped the necklace and tugged at the chain even as she pulled away from him. In an instant, the delicate necklace broke causing her to topple backward. To Adriana's surprise, the viscount's fist flashed as she fell, landing squarely on the highwayman's jaw. But there was no time for celebration when the thief crumpled to the dirt. As his lordship turned to her, an accomplice stepped from the mists behind him.

"Watch out—" was all Adriana had time to cry before a great cudgel came down on Lord Borland's head, knocking him senseless. He fell to the ground beside her, and she scrambled to him, still on her knees. Blood poured from the wound onto the white snow. She knew something must be done at once to stop the flow or he would likely bleed to death. She grabbed the end of her cape and pressed the wool fabric against the wound.

Anger caused her to throw caution to the wind. "If he dies, we'll see you all hanged, you blackguards."

The first highwayman, back on his feet, rubbed his jaw. "Serves his lordship right for tryin' to draw me cork—" but he never got to finish his sentence.

Off the roof of the carriage a tiny body flew with fists flying. The lad landed on the highwayman's head, knocking off his hat and exposing reddish-blond hair. Nick flailed at the thief's face with his small hands, but he was no match for the grown man and was quickly hurled to the ground. To everyone's surprise, the boy managed to hang on to the man's mask, ripping it from the villain's face.

"I've a good mind to let daylight into ye, ye little whelp." Completely oblivious of the fact his countenance was visible, he focused all his anger on the lad.

Adriana watched in horror as the highwayman drew a bead on the boy. Without a thought to her own safety, she pulled from her reticule the small pistol she'd been hiding and aimed at the highwayman's chest. "I shall shoot if you don't leave here at once."

The villain eyed the small gun, then looked into the lady's dark eyes. He saw no weakness or hesitation, only fury. It never paid to trifle with a woman when she was in a black rage, as this one was right now, he thought. With a nod to the accomplice at the rear of the coach, he shouted, "Let's ride."

As quickly as it had begun, it was over. The shadowy figures disappeared into the fog, then the clattering of hooves could be heard thundering away into the distance. Adriana stuffed the small gun back into her reticule and turned her attention back to the viscount as Thomas and Jock came to stand over their employer.

But Nick stared in amazement at the young lady. "Where'd ye find that barker, miss?"

As she reapplied pressure to William's wound, she replied, "Italy is full of *banditi*. One would never travel without protection. The gun was a gift from my father years ago."

Thomas, while impressed with the young lady's pluck, was more worried about Lord Borland. "Is he hurt bad, Miss Addington?"

"I fear so, Thomas. How far are we from his lordship's home? Or would an inn be closer? We must find him a doctor at once."

Jock said, "We're but a few miles from the abbey, miss."

"Then we must hurry."

With that, the servants who'd been in something of a stunned stupor sprang into action. The footman and coachman lifted William into the carriage, laying him on the seat, his head in Adriana's lap. As the carriage moved at an unsafe speed for the conditions, she prayed they would make it to his lordship's estate in one piece, and the doctor might be summoned posthaste.

An urgent pounding on the front door of Borwood Abbey startled Mrs. Raines, the housekeeper, as she sat enjoying a simple tea in her rooms with the only other servant at the hall she deemed her equal. Having been employed some years, the woman had become something of a taskmaster in the opinion of those who worked under her, but his lordship remained unaware of her domineering nature, for she ran his house smoothly, rarely disrupting his life. She looked at the butler, Curtwood, with her brows raised. "Whoever can that be making such a ruckus with his lordship gone?"

The lady was quick to learn who when she and the butler arrived in the front hall. The footman on duty opened the door and a veritable legion of people streamed into the marble-floored entry. To the housekeeper's way of thinking, there were a great many females in the group. A pretty young lady Mrs. Raines had never before set eyes upon barked orders at the viscount's servants to be careful of the gentleman they held.

Drawing herself up, prepared to do battle with this presumptuous female who'd invaded his lordship's home, the wind rushed from Mrs. Raines's lungs as she saw the new coachman, Jock, and Thomas standing in the doorway with anxious eyes. A chill raced down her spine. They'd left with the viscount some six days before and now they were returned. But where was his lordship? The woman's gaze flew to the man who lay unconscious, but she couldn't see past the footmen who crowded around the man. For the first time she noted a child near the woman.

"Who is in charge here?" Adriana asked. There seemed to be servants everywhere, but none did more than gape at their master.

A gray-haired gentleman with a slight limp stepped forward and bowed. "I'm Curtwood, Lord Borland's butler."

"His lordship's been struck unconscious by a highwayman. You must send for the doctor at once." Adriana vaguely took note of a dimly lit cavernous anteroom as two ancient retainers came through the sea of parting footmen. But the pair were as shocked into inactivity at the sight of his lordship's condition as Thomas and Jock had been on the roadway. Clearly, the viscount's people rarely had to deal with emergencies. As the old butler stared mutely down at Lord Borland, Adriana snapped, "At once, Curtwood!"

The housekeeper seemed to awaken from her stunned surprise first. "Bring his lordship upstairs."

Adriana trailed behind the footmen who carried the still-unconscious lord up the marble stairs and down an unlit hallway. Mrs. Raines's brace of candles illuminated a wide hall lined with portraits as she led the way. Soon they came to his lordship's apartments, and the men laid the wounded man gently on the great fourposter. The housekeeper set one of the footmen to make a fire as she lit the candles in the room, then she took note that one of the young ladies had followed them.

"Who are you, miss?" There was a bristling quality to her tone. Mrs. Raines, having served the viscount faithfully for over fifteen years, saw herself as something of a protector of the gentleman's privacy. Especially now in his weakened state. Over the years there had been various attempts by young ladies to gain access to Lord Borland's home with rather flimsy excuses to make the acquaintance of a wealthy, handsome viscount.

Adriana, unaware of the housekeeper's suspicions, removed her bonnet as she went to stand beside his lordship. "I am Miss Adriana Addington, Lady Margaret's companion. Lord Borland was escorting me to Scotland, when we were waylaid by brigands in the woods near here." She thought the gentleman looked frighteningly pale, and she knew it was her fault. If only she hadn't struggled when the blackguard had tried to rob her, Borland wouldn't have felt the need to defend her.

"And the other women in the hall?" Mrs. Raines well knew his lordship's thoughts on females invading the abbey and had been as stunned by their appearance as by the gentleman's injury.

" 'Tis a long story, Mrs. . . ."

"Raines. I am his lordship's housekeeper."

"Do you not think we should remove Lord Borland's bloody clothes before the doctor arrives?" Adriana leaned forward and tugged at the intricately knotted cravat, wanting only to do all in her power to help.

"Miss Addington!" the housekeeper said in shocked tones as she hurried to the bed. *"I* shall see to his lordship. I know Lady Margaret has great plans for her grandson, but you'll not be pulling any unseemly tricks while I have breath. It's not proper for an unmarried female to be undressing a gentleman, and so I'll tell the countess when I see her again. Do go to the drawing room, miss, and I shall see that you and the other guests have refreshments sent as soon as is possible."

Adriana blushed at the housekeeper's insinuation that she was in some way trying to compromise herself. She hadn't given the matter of helping the least thought. Having nursed both her mother and father through long illness, she simply reacted. Her mind had been too full of her worries about the viscount to think about silly proprieties. But she could see the housekeeper was determined to see her gone before a single thing was done.

"Very well, Mrs. Raines, I shall leave you to the matter. But first I will have you know I am not in a plot with her ladyship, since I never set eyes on the countess in my life."

With that, Adriana turned and went to the door, her head held high. About to exit, she turned and with as much dignity as possible added, "I should very much like to speak with the doctor after he has seen Lord Borland."

Reluctantly, Adriana made her way back to the front hall, guided by the footman who'd finished with the fire. She was then ushered into a small drawing room, where a fire had been lit for the visitors. Nancy hurried to her as she entered the room.

"That Curtwood fellow showed me your rooms, miss. Let me take you up and remove that bloody dress."

Adriana looked down and discovered that her blue traveling gown was saturated. The sheer size of the stain only made her more frightened for Lord Borland's life. Her mind raced with all the possibilities of what would happen if his lordship were to die. Lady Margaret would blame herself, having asked Borland to make the journey.

Katy and Nick might be tossed out by the viscount's cousin. But worst of all would be Adriana's own guilt.

Hearing a sniffle, Adriana was drawn from her worries by the sight of Thomas trying to comfort the beautiful Katy, who was once again quietly weeping near the fireplace. At the moment, Adriana was too tired and too heartsick to deal with the girl's hysterics, so she allowed Nancy to lead her back out and up the stairs. As she reached the landing, she paused. "Where is Nick?"

"Don't you be worryin' your head about that young scamp. Jock took him to the stables. The lad protested loudly, wanting to stay and see how the viscount fared, but we didn't think you'd want the child underfoot just now."

Adriana merely nodded as they entered a large chamber with green and yellow hangings. "I must change quickly. I want to speak to the doctor when he arrives. I must know how his lordship is doing. Oh, Nancy, what if he dies and all because of me?"

"What nonsense, miss. He would have done as much for any one of us, and that I know. He's just that kind of honorable man. Now, lift your arms and let me take off that gown. I'll have you clean and dressed afore that sawbones has even begun to look at his lordship."

And the maid was as good as her word. Adriana returned to the drawing room to find the chamber empty. A simple repast awaited her on the table, but she couldn't eat. She felt certain that Thomas had seen to Katy's comfort, so there was nothing left for her to do but await the doctor. But being quite alone made the time seem to drag, and Adriana began to pace the Aubusson rug as the clock ticked loudly on the mantelpiece. After some twenty minutes, a rotund gentleman with thinning red hair and a too small waistcoat strolled into the chamber. He took more note of the cold collation Mrs. Raines had set upon the table than of the occupant of the room.

The housekeeper stood at the door, her hands crossed primly. "Miss Addington, this is Dr. Burrell."

In a rush, Adriana asked, "How is his lordship?"

"Ah, I've been without a meal all day, what with one thing and another." With that, he picked up a slice of bread and began to butter it as if the young lady hadn't uttered a word.

Adriana stepped forward, fear gripping her heart. "Doctor, how is Lord Borland?"

Slapping a slice of ham on the bread, the man folded it over and took a huge bite. Then he held up a hand to let the young lady know he would answer in a moment. Those few moments were the longest in Adriana's life. At last, after drinking a sip of the tea that Mrs. Raines came forward and poured for him, he said, "It looks much worse than it is, Miss Addington. Head wounds always bleed frightfully, but that's not to say it's not serious. Have you a spot of brandy to warm up this brew, Mrs. Raines?"

The housekeeper retrieved a bottle from a side table and poured a generous portion into the doctor's cup.

Adriana was growing impatient. "Has Lord Borland regained his wits, Doctor?"

"Not yet, and I shan't leave until he does. Have you any of those little lemon cakes you are so famous for, Mrs. Raines?"

The housekeeper signaled a footman, and with a word in his ear sent the fellow scurrying.

Adriana's impatience turned to anger, but she bit her tongue to keep from lashing out at the infuriating physician. That gentleman seemed far more concerned with his palate than with the viscount's condition. "But will his lordship recover? Do you think there will be any permanent damage, sir?"

Burrell took another bite and seemed to contemplate the question as he chewed. "He's young and in good health. Gave a few hardy groans as I bandaged his head, which is a promising sign. I'd say if he wakes before morning, which is very likely, then I'll expect a full recovery."

Adriana sank onto a red and gold striped sofa, her knees suddenly going weak from relief. She told herself that her reaction came from concern about her ladyship's only grandson, but deep inside she knew that she liked the viscount, and far more than was safe for her own well-being. This gentleman she found herself caring more for as each day passed wasn't in search of a wife, and she'd best remember that.

In an instinctive movement, she reached up for her gold charm before remembering it was no longer there. In all the excitement, she'd completely forgotten that the highwayman had stolen her necklace. Was it an omen that she might never find her heart's desire? Was she destined to spend her days as a companion, never to know true happiness? She genuinely hoped the loss of her keepsake was just a momentary stroke of bad luck and nothing more.

Pain radiated in William's head from back to front. He felt as if he were in a great fog and must fight his way to the light. Was he sick? He had a vague memory of speaking with Dr. Burrell, but the image hovered hazily in his mind. With a great effort he finally opened his eyes and to his amazement discovered himself in his chamber at Borwood Abbey. How had he gotten there?

He searched his memory, but the last thing he remembered was being in the carriage with Miss Addington, Katy Hunt, and Nancy. Had there been an accident? Were the ladies injured as well? Or had he merely succumbed to some malady?

He tried to rise, but the world began to spin. He closed

his eyes for a moment, then reopened them, and everything had righted itself. After a moment his head no longer throbbed, just held to a steady ache.

A snuffling snore startled him and his gaze traveled the room. He spied a female asleep in a wing chair beside the hearth. He recognized her as the upstairs maid. Peggy, he thought. But before he could reason out her being there, his door softly creaked open.

A small blond head popped around the oak door, and a great grin split a freckled face. Nick's gaze darted to Peggy, and he put his finger to his lips as he closed the door quietly behind him. Then he tiptoed across the room and climbed up on the viscount's bed. The process made the bed shake, and the jarring reminded William that he had a frightful headache. Raising his hand to his temple, he discovered there was a large bandage wrapped around his head.

"Ain't supposed to be 'ere, m'lord. That Raines mort done threatened to part me 'air with a stool if I disturb ye, but I 'ad to see as 'ow ye was truly awake like that sawbones said."

Despite the returned throb in his head, William smiled as he dropped his hand back to the bed. He was weak as a newborn kitten. "That is just why I employ the lady. But 'tis happy I am to see you, lad, with your scalp in one piece. Mayhap you can tell me how I came to be here and with a dreadful headache."

"Ye don't remember? Don't surprise me, what with 'aving yer nob bashed. Well, there was some coves on the high pad and ye planted a facer on one of 'em for takin' Miss Addington's gold bauble, but another one cupled ye on the nob. Just then the young lady pulled out 'er barking iron and puts the lot of 'em in the pike." Nick grinned as he finished the tale.

It took a moment for the viscount to interpret the cant, but at last he realized they'd been set upon by highwaymen. He'd been knocked out and the most unbelievable part was that Miss Addington had produced a pistol from somewhere and frightened the fellows away. His mind reeled at the very thought of a female wielding a gun.

But before his pain-racked mind could make any sense of what Nick had just told him, the door opened and Mrs. Raines entered. Upon seeing Nick perched on his lordship's bed, the housekeeper's gaunt cheeks puffed out and her lips thinned. She made for the lad without delay and grabbed him by the ear. "What are you doing in here, boy? Did I not tell you—"

"Mrs. Raines, there is no harm done." William put his hand on Nick, and the woman released her hold on the boy's ear, but she continued to glare at the child.

"You mustn't be disturbed, my lord. Dr. Burrell said you need to stay abed and sleep for at least several days." As if the physician's orders negated the viscount's wishes, she tugged the lad down from the bed and kept a firm grip upon his shoulder.

A bit piqued at having his order remanded, William snapped, "I shall be better when I have all the facts about how I received my injury, Mrs. Raines, which the lad has been giving me."

"Well, my lord, as *I* see the facts, your grandmother has managed to lure you to Wother Castle for the holidays despite your wishes, which has resulted in your nearly being killed. The doctor has rushed off in the middle of the night to deliver a set of twins, leaving you with only that worthless Peg to watch over you." The housekeeper gestured to the sleeping maid. "Then there is Lady Underhill and her daughter, who have called twice this morning trying to discover news of you, but if you ask me . . ."

The viscount closed his eyes. Every time he thought he'd gotten rid of the baroness and her beautiful but vacuous daughter, they found some new excuse to once again plague him. His head ached and he felt too tired to worry about any unwanted visitors, so he let Mrs. Raines continue her tirade unchecked.

". . . and the magistrate sent word he shall be here at eleven sharp to question everyone about the robbery. And as if that weren't enough, there is this odd collection of females you brought, one flirting with all the footmen, one trying to tell me how to manage this establishment, and one practically haunting the hall in front of your door since first light."

On that, William opened his eyes. "Is Miss Addington just outside?"

The housekeeper stopped and puckered her mouth sourly. "Not at present, my lord. I was able to send her to the breakfast parlor, where she belonged. You might rest peacefully knowing that *I* shan't allow you to be disturbed by some pushing chit."

William wondered if Mrs. Raines had always been this dictatorial, or had he merely disconcerted her with his unconventional arrival. It wasn't every day that he was brought home unconscious. That made him think of the robbery, and he remembered Nick's tale of a pistol and the lady's heroism. He was very curious what Miss Addington would have to say about the events.

"I must speak with the lady. When she finishes her meal, please ask her to join me here." He paused a minute, then added, "And remember the lady is a guest in my home."

Mrs. Raines harrumphed softly but merely said, "As you wish, my lord. And what of the boy?" Her indignant gaze returned to Nick, who had wiggled free of the woman's restraining hand and moved to inspect a set of crossed Spanish swords on the wall during the housekeeper's diatribe.

"Leave him with me for the moment. He and I shall discuss his duties."

"Might I recommend the stables as the best place for the lad, my lord?"

Nick, who'd suddenly become aware he was being discussed, watched the woman with a hint of defiance in his green eyes. "Ain't sleepin' with no prads. Like 'em well enough, but don't want to be beddin' down with 'em, not with me new clean rig."

Seeing the displeasure on his housekeeper's face, William decided he'd best take matters in hand. Clearly, the lady had taken the lad in dislike and might be a bit harsh with him if her current attitude was any indication.

"I think I shall make Nick my personal footman when I travel. Please see that he is dressed in proper livery later, Mrs. Raines. That will be all for now."

It looked for a moment like the woman would protest, but at last she turned to leave.

"Oh, and you may take Peggy with you. I shan't need anyone to sit with me again."

Her back rigid with dissatisfaction at having her wishes disregarded, the woman marched around the end of the bed to the fireplace. It was an unwelcome surprise to her to have his lordship take an interest in his servants. She and Curtwood had always had complete control. She stalked up to the sleeping maid and cuffed the girl on the head, nearly knocking off her mobcap. "Wake up, you noddy. I may as well have put a suit of armor in here to watch over Lord Borland for all your lack of vigilance."

After the housekeeper and maid left, the viscount called Nick back to his bedside. He began to explain what the boy's duties would be and found Nick perfectly agreeable. He made the lad promise to keep out from underfoot in the kitchens, or Mrs. Raines would be banishing him to the stables yet.

"Am I to have one of them fancy red uniforms what

the lads in the 'all wears, with the bright silver buttons?" The boy's eyes glowed with anticipation.

The viscount smiled at the description of his servants' apparel. "I believe claret would best describe the color. And yes, you shall have a new set of clothes, but you must promise to take care of them."

Nick gave a shout of delight, but seeing his lordship grimace in pain at the loud noise, he settled down at once. "Didn't mean to 'urt yer nob, m'lord. I just ain't never had more 'un one set a duds in me life and nothin' so fine as a uniform."

"Well, young man, your first duty is to go and escort Miss Addington from the breakfast parlor, but not until she has finished her meal."

Nick straightened and gave his lordship a military salute. "Yes, m'lord." He hurried to the door, then stopped to grin at his employer. "I seen a soldier do that once and always wanted to do it meself. Now I 'as me own red uniform, so I can."

Despite the continued pain in his head, William laughed as the lad exited the room. Nick was a disruption with his chatter and incessant curiosity, but the young boy had a certain naive appeal. Even knowing the boy was likely to create mischief on occasion, the viscount didn't regret that they rescued him. The reflection of what his life would have been was too dark to contemplate. And if he became too much of a disturbance in the house, he could turn him over to Jock to train.

Then his thoughts turned to the young lady. That brought a pucker to the viscount's forehead that had nothing to do with the pain inside. What the devil had an impulsive young female been doing carrying a loaded pistol? But somehow he knew that the stalwart Miss Addington would have a perfectly good explanation. Or at least one that would be perfectly logical to her.

With that, he closed his eyes to await the arrival of

his grandmother's companion. It suddenly struck him that he wanted to see her very much, not just to hear her account of events but to know that she'd survived their ordeal with no harm. Despite his best intentions, he was finding that the lady's well-being had become rather important to him.

Seven

The abbey appeared strangely quiet that morning. It was as if every servant were waiting with fearful anticipation to hear how his lordship was before daily duties began. Adriana sat alone in a small breakfast parlor with beautiful arched windows that overlooked a snow-covered garden. The viscount's disapproving housekeeper had shown her there after she'd gone to his lordship's rooms to discover how the gentleman had passed the night. She couldn't quite determine what it was about her that Mrs. Raines disliked, but clearly the housekeeper wanted Adriana gone from Borwood Abbey at the earliest possible moment. The woman had denied Adriana access to Lord Borland even as she announced that the doctor had said his lordship had awakened during the night and was well on the road to recovery.

Before leaving the breakfast parlor, the housekeeper informed Adriana the magistrate was coming to interview her about the robbery. She was not to wander about the house or to disturb Lord Borland. With that surly announcement, the woman had departed.

With little appetite and Mrs. Raines's restrictions ringing in her ears, Adriana toyed with her meal. She debated whether she should write Lady Margaret about the reason for their delay, then decided against it as she watched new snowflakes begin to fall. Hearing about her grandson's injury would only upset the lady. Perhaps it was better to allow the countess to assume the wintry weather was the reason they hadn't arrived. Likely his lordship would be better soon, and they could resume their journey if the snow ceased, then his grandmother wouldn't have to worry.

Some twenty minutes later the door to the parlor flew open and in bounced Nick. "Are ye done eatin', miss? 'Is lordship be wantin' to see ye upstairs when ye's finished." He tugged on her arm, not at all the proper servant.

She pushed the plate of half-eaten buttered eggs and toast aside. "I am ready, Nick. Take me to Lord Borland." She didn't dally since she knew that if the housekeeper arrived, the old tartar would try to stop them both from going upstairs.

When they reached the door to the viscount's chamber, Adriana stopped to nervously smooth the wrinkles from her simple lilac morning gown and pat her dark curls to make certain everything was still neatly in place. She didn't know why, but she wanted to look her best when he saw her.

"Ye's pretty as a daisy, miss."

She grinned at the boy. "You shall make me quite conceited, young man."

Nick didn't know what she meant, but he thought the lady could be anything she liked as far as he was concerned. Then he realized he'd best warn her about the viscount. " 'Is lordship's brains is a bit scrambled, miss."

"What do you mean?"

" 'E don't remember nothin' 'bout what 'appened during the robbery. I 'ad to tell 'im everythin'."

Adriana patted young Nick's shoulder. "I don't think that is unusual when someone is knocked unconscious. Very often their memory returns later." She wondered briefly exactly what the imaginative Nick had told his lordship.

After a knock, the pair entered to find Borland sitting up in bed. A neat white bandage bound his head, leaving his sandy-brown hair more tousled than Nick's. He looked so boyishly handsome that Adriana felt a strange thumping of her heart. Ignoring the sensation, she found herself reassured that his face held more color than the last time she'd seen him. His blue gaze appeared to lock on her with a speculative gleam, as if he weren't quite sure what to expect from her. Hysterics or melodramatics about the frightening event? Well, he would discover that she was made of sterner stuff than that.

"Good morning, Miss Addington." William was surprised to see the lady looking much as she always did, perhaps with a shade more concern in her eyes. Should not a genteel female be showing some signs of the ordeal she'd just survived?

"Good morning, my lord."

"Nick, my housekeeper tells me that the magistrate is coming. Go to the window and keep a watch for his carriage. He drives a black gig with a set of matched grays." The viscount wanted the boy out of the way during the interview. He knew the lad had an excessive fondness for his benefactress.

Nick gave a quick salute, which caused Adriana to smile, then he hurried to the set of oriel windows at the opposite end of the room and perched on the window seat.

"Pray have a seat, Miss Addington. There is something I wish to discuss with you." The viscount gestured to the wing chair that sat at the end of the bed. After she was settled, he continued. "So, how have you fared after this frightening experience?" He quirked one brown brow.

"Me? I wasn't harmed in the least, nor any of the other women. Although Katy did suffer a nervous upset, but she became quite content after we reached the abbey.

'Tis you, my lord, we have all been greatly worried about."

"You may assure them I shall be fine." He was quiet a moment, but his gaze never left her face. "I understand from Nick that we were waylaid on the road. More important, he told me you were carrying a pistol and frightened off the highwaymen."

There was something in Borland's look that suggested he was less than pleased about the matter. Tilting her chin upward, she replied, "I was armed my lord, and I did frighten off the men. I have always traveled with a pistol, as did my father, brother, and sister. Italy was a very dangerous place when outside *Roma.*"

His lordship's mouth thinned. "Do you think that is safe? Females carrying weapons in their reticules?"

"I do. Did your coachman not have a pistol in his driving cape?"

"But, Miss Addington, that is quite different. All coachmen carry pistols and, after all, he is a man."

She laughed. "Do you think women incapable of handling a weapon? Perhaps you should read a bit more about women in history, my lord."

The viscount made a dismissive gesture with his hand. "I know there have been those rare females who made a name for themselves in battle, like Joan of Arc, but you must remember there are many who thought her quite mad or dabbling in the black arts. I am thinking of women on a more practical, modern level. Few of them would wish to own a pistol, and fewer still have been trained in their safety and handling."

"Well, my lord, I have had both." Adriana glanced to where Nick sat, drawing pictures on the frosted windowpanes. She lowered her voice. "Lord Borland, had I not had that small gun my father gave me *and* trained me to use, Nick might not be here with us at this very moment."

Doubt reflected in the depths of the gentleman's blue eyes as he glanced toward the small boy. "Would you have me believe that a highwayman, no matter how dastardly, would shoot a mere child?"

She folded her hands and sat back, realizing that Nick must have given his lordship a very edited version of what had occurred. "He would indeed, if the child, after having seen his beloved master struck senseless, had just leapt from the box, knocked off the highwayman's hat, pummeled his face, and stripped off his mask."

The viscount's gaze moved to Nick again, a startled expression on his face. "The little lad did that?"

"Most decisively."

Borland sat in silence for a moment, a half-smile on his face. Suddenly his features sobered and his gaze returned to Adriana. "Still, I cannot like the idea of *females* being armed in carriages. It just isn't safe."

From the window seat Nick shouted, "Carriage comin' up the drive, m'lord. And 'tis beginnin' to snow hard again."

The viscount winced and pressed his fingers to his temples as the boy climbed down and dashed back to the bed. "Please, lad, my head."

"Sorry, m'lord, I forgot."

Adriana, piqued at his lordship's attitude about her pistol, rose. "Well, my lord, I must go and give an account of what happened for the magistrate, but first I must say I think it unfair of you to speak of females as if we were all exactly alike, flighty and hysterical at the least sign of danger. Do you think yourself exactly like every other man you have met?"

"Hardly." It had been his experience that he was considered an oddity among the *ton* even now, despite the fact, or because of the fact, that he rarely went to public affairs.

"Then why is it that you would see women as coming

only in one type? And a type, I might add, that is less than flattering to most of us."

At that moment a knock sounded at the door. Mrs. Raines entered. "Squire Longworth is here, my lord, wishing to speak about the robbery." Then her gaze landed on Nick. "As for you, young man, the seamstress is awaiting you in the sewing room to measure you for your uniform."

Nick dashed out the door in a flash. His footsteps could be heard echoing down the stairs.

Without waiting for a response to her query from the viscount, Adriana moved to the door. Then she turned before exiting, her face a mask of cool affront. "I hope you are feeling more the thing quite soon, my lord. I shall inform the magistrate you are unavailable at the moment and have no memory of the events."

Realizing that he'd let his prejudice cause him to un-intentionally insult her instead of thanking her for what she'd done, William called, "Miss Addington, you were quite right. I made an unfair assumption about you simply because you are female. Will you forgive me?"

The young lady merely nodded her head, aware that the housekeeper stood beside her, all ears.

"Would you"—the viscount hesitated, then continued—"or do I ask too much, read to me this evening?"

First he saw a look of surprise, then that delightful twinkle returned to her amber gaze. "I will, my lord. But you cannot fool me. You are quite determined to turn me into a reader yet."

With that she left the room. Mrs. Raines stood for a moment, eyeing the viscount with a bemused expression seeming to want to say something. But instead she shrugged as she closed the door. William, paying little heed to his housekeeper, wondered what had come over him. Why the devil had he asked Miss Addington to read to him?

His thoughts returned to their conversation and her accusation that he thought all women were alike. He knew he couldn't deny that. His experiences with his family and in London had perhaps given him a somewhat unvaried view of females. Yet he had proof daily that Miss Addington was nothing like those flighty women he'd met in London so long ago. True, she wasn't a great reader, but he never found her conversations boring.

He lay his still-aching head back on the pillow. Then he smiled, perhaps he was trying to turn the unconventional Miss Addington into a reader. Wouldn't that be nice?

The magistrate, Squire Longworth, was the worst kind of dandy—an aging one. He rarely paid much heed to his official duties. It was unusual to find someone of his station so much involved in social affairs, but his own father had invested wisely, leaving a considerable fortune on his death at the age of ninety. Now Longworth was determined to purchase himself a baronet's title, and he'd penned his hopes on Lord Borland helping. With that in mind, he hurried to the abbey on being informed of the robbery.

As Adriana and Nancy, who had been awaiting the young lady in the front hall on Mrs. Raines's urging, arrived in the drawing room, they discovered a gentleman in his late fifties. He was dressed in his voluminous driving coat, one side of which was tossed back over his shoulder, exposing the red silk lining. At present he stood before the room's only looking glass, turning from side to side, tugging on first one thing, then adjusting another to suit him.

His sparse gray hair was dressed à la Titus in an attempt to minimize a balding spot at the back. His willow-green superfine coat strained at its oversized mother-of-pearl buttons over his round belly and marigold waistcoat. His Hessian boots with gold tassels gleamed, save where he had trudged through the snow to come indoors.

Eyeing the foppish fellow, Adriana suddenly realized for the first time that it was unlikely the local law would ever find the highwayman who'd waylaid them. With a sigh, she stepped forward, a smile she was far from feeling pasted on her face.

"Good morning, sir. I am Miss Adriana Addington, and this is my maid, Nancy Ross. We are at present guests of Lord Borland's and were with him during the robbery yesterday."

The gentleman lifted his quizzing glass, then squinted his eyes to take a better look at the females. He'd heard rumors Borland had brought a bevy of females to the abbey. Vanity kept him from giving in to age and wearing glasses, but he thought the tall brunette passably pretty from what he could discern. The maid he paid little heed to.

He swept her a bow with a driving cape grand enough for the king, which almost caused Adriana to giggle. She was certain she'd never seen such an absurd gesture before.

"Good morning, Miss Addington." The squire straightened, then peered myopically behind her. "Where is the viscount?"

"Did you not know that his lordship was injured during the robbery, sir?"

"Egad, that's cursed bad luck. I suppose I shan't be able to tell the constable anything until his lordship recovers his good health." With that, the gentleman retrieved his gloves from the nearby table and began to put them on, intending to depart without a single question to the women. In truth, the gentleman cared little about the event, wanting only to impress the viscount with his vigilance.

Adriana and Nancy exchanged a knowing look. Why was it that so many men assumed women were addlepated? Adriana asked, "Do you not wish to hear what we have to tell you, sir?"

"Especially since we got to see one of the brigand's faces," Nancy added curtly, "which his lordship did not, since he was already struck down by then."

Longworth paused in what he was doing. It wouldn't look good if one of these females told his lordship that the magistrate hadn't taken an interest. "Saw one of 'em, did you? What did the blackguard look like?"

"Well, he had—" Adriana began, but Nancy interrupted.

"Why don't you draw the villain's picture, miss? You're an excellent artist."

"A capital suggestion, miss, if you think you can do a reasonable rendition." The squire cast a quick glance in the looking glass and straightened a gray curl above his ear.

"I can, sir." Adriana went to a small rosewood secretary that stood against the blue-moiré-silk-covered wall as Nancy filled in the magistrate about the events of the previous evening. Adriana drew out a piece of vellum and found a small pencil which she sharpened with a knife.

She quickly began the sketch. As she worked, Squire Longworth and Nancy moved to stand behind her, watching the process as the gentleman tossed out the random question about the incident. Adriana had just started on the villain's evil-looking eyes, when an arrival could be heard in the hall. Within minutes the drawing room door opened and a large aging female swathed in purple trimmed with sable and a petite blonde in rose pink with a black spencer edged with pink swansdown strolled into the room.

The older woman, in a booming voice, called, "So,

Longworth, I see you managed to pull yourself from in front of your dressing table long enough to do your duty. About time, I must say. The neighborhood isn't safe with brigands striking down our most prominent citizens."

"Lady Underhill, Miss Underhill, delighted." Squire Longworth spoke in a tone that expressed more disgust than delight. To Adriana's amazement, she heard the gentleman add under his breath, "You old dragon."

"Where is Borland?" her ladyship demanded as her intense gaze swept the room. "I insist on seeing him at once. We must observe for ourselves that he is truly unharmed. Janetta didn't manage a wink of sleep last night worrying about her dear Borland."

Adriana thought the young lady looked surprisingly bright-eyed for a sleep-deprived female. Suddenly behind her, the magistrate muttered, "More likely plotting how to intrude here, the little jade." Then he turned to Adriana and said in a normal but hurried tone, "I've just remembered I must speak with the local constable at once, Miss Addington. When you've completed your drawing, have a footman bring it to me at Longly Manor."

With that and a curt nod to the two females who'd just entered, the gentleman departed.

As the front door banged shut, the maid exchanged a puzzled look with Adriana. They both were left to wonder what had caused the squire to suddenly dash out. Was the gentleman afraid of Lady Underhill? Or was it merely intense dislike that caused his hasty departure?

Adriana bit at her lip. She was in something of a quandary at the moment. Lord Borland had not empowered her to act as his hostess, yet Lady Underhill stood staring at her with a curious yet hostile gaze. Realizing she must do something, Adriana rose and curtsied politely. "Good morning, my lady."

"Who are you, gel?"

Adriana had never felt more unfashionable in her life

as her ladyship's cool gaze raked her up and down. But while she didn't have the title, her bloodlines were excellent. "I am Miss Adriana Addington, Lady Margaret's new companion. Lord Borland was kindly escorting her ladyship's maid and me to Scotland for the holidays when the robbery occurred."

"She sent a maid to act as companion for a mere servant? What extravagance, but then, so like the countess." With that the lady lifted a lorgnette to peer at Adriana. "Or perhaps she was protecting the viscount from the dangers of foolish young women who aspire above their station."

Adriana was outraged. Suddenly all her good judgment fled and she became determined to rid the house of this veritable dragon as soon as possible. "Lady Underhill, Lord Borland is not yet receiving visitors. Was there something else you wished, or shall I have Nancy escort you to the door?"

But Lady Underhill was not to be so easily routed. "Of course we cannot depart. The road was nearly impassable as we came from Hillsborough. There is no possibility we could return safely home at present. Janetta and I shall have to remain through the afternoon. If things do not improve, no doubt Borland will insist we stay the night."

There was a smug glow on the lady's lined face, but beside her Miss Underhill seemed more interested in taking an inventory of the small items on a nearby table. Without a word, the young lady duly followed her mother to a blue damask sofa in front of the fire, but instead of taking a seat with her mother, she began to inspect the figurines on the mantel.

Having no intention of staying to entertain the rude Lady Underhill and her nosy daughter, Adriana said, "Then, madam, you must discuss your arrangements with Mrs. Raines. Pray, excuse me, but I have important matters awaiting my attention. Come, Nancy." Adriana picked up her drawing and departed the chamber.

In the hall she stopped. "Nancy, you must inform Mrs. Raines of his lordship's newest guests. I fear for my safety to be the bearer of such bad tidings."

Nancy chuckled, "Ah, the old sayin' about kill the messenger, you mean."

"Just so."

After Nancy departed for the kitchens, Adriana made her way up to her room. Lady Underhill had done something no other person had, not even his lordship. Her cutting remark had made Adriana finally realize that her life in England would be different from anything she had known. She was no longer perceived as the genteel daughter of noble lineage but instead an impoverished female who must earn her living. Most would consider her an upper servant but a servant all the same. Even Lord Borland had referred to her as such during the robbery. It was a very lowering thought for the granddaughter of a count.

Adriana had never given much thought to marriage, just assuming that like most women, one day she would wed. But in her current station, she wasn't likely to find many gentlemen who would form an alliance with a lady's companion. On that dark thought, she entered her room to finish the drawing for Squire Longworth. At least she had her talent, which no matter how low her station, she would always possess.

For the remainder of the afternoon Adriana stayed in her room. Signora, her only companion, lay curled up on the large bed without a care in the world. The feline had been the only female Mrs. Raines had welcomed with open arms. She had given the cat free run of the abbey.

Deciding there was no point in wallowing in self-pity at the realization of her lowered circumstances, Adriana set aside her pique at Mrs. Raines as well as at the arrogant Lady Underhill and her daughter. After all, she wasn't likely to see the ladies once they departed Borwood.

She worked diligently on her drawing of the highwayman for much of the afternoon. With each clean stroke of her pencil she knew she wanted this man to suffer punishment for what he'd done to Lord Borland. Also there was the matter of her necklace. Was it lost to her forever?

At last, thinking she had a reasonable rendition of the villainous man, she summoned Nancy for her opinion. The maid agreed that she'd captured the fellow exactly, and so a footman was set to carry the picture to Squire Longworth in the morning if the roads were clear. With that done, Adriana found time weighed heavily on her hands. Once again alone, she moved to the windows. The snow had ceased to fall, and a break in the clouds had suddenly turned his lordship's garden into a sparkling winter wonderland. The pristine blanket of snow inspired her.

Adriana got out her sketchbook and worked until the sun sank behind the trees. As usual when she worked, time had no meaning and she was startled when Nancy arrived, saying it was time to dress for dinner.

"Dinner?" Adriana suddenly wished she were brave enough to ask Mrs. Raines to set a tray for her in Lord Borland's room while he ate, but she knew that would put her beyond the pale with the woman. "Must I dress if I am dining alone?"

"Alone? You won't be alone. Her ladyship's coachman wandered up from the stables and positively vows that the roads are impassable even though a flake ain't fallen in the last three hours. If you ask me, the fellow was coached, but it ain't like Mrs. Raines could toss them out. So, they must stay the night." Nancy sniffed, showing what she thought of the situation even as she went to the wardrobe to fetch the young lady's evening gown.

Adriana puckered her face at the thought of dining with the baroness but made no comment. Perhaps, she thought, she would find that Miss Underhill was more congenial than her mother. Then a smile lit her face as she remembered that Lord Borland had asked her to read to him that evening.

At last dressed in her only evening gown, a rose-pink silk gown trimmed with ivory ribbons and lace that Amy had made out of one of their mother's old gowns, Adriana lingered in her room long after she'd dismissed Nancy. She waited until the gong sounded. She knew she was being rude, but the less time she spent under Lady Underhill's inhospitable gaze, the happier Adriana would be.

Making her way down the hall, she came upon a maid and Mrs. Raines in conversation. The girl held a tray that Adriana could only assume was his lordship's evening meal.

"But he says he won't have no gruel, Mrs. Raines. Said to take it back to the kitchens and bring him a beef-steak and ale. He has only the headache, not the ague."

The housekeeper put her hands upon her hips, unaware of Adriana's approach. "Well, take that bowl right back and tell him it's not gruel. 'Tis only barley broth with a bit of beef and bread, which is what Dr. Burrell ordered."

The young servant bobbed a curtsy and hurried back up the hall. Just then the housekeeper turned and spied Adriana coming toward her. Perhaps the woman was merely distracted, or perhaps she was warming to his lordship's guest, but she gave a half-smile, saying, "You are looking quite lovely this evening, Miss Addington."

Hoping to convince the woman she had no evil designs

on the viscount, Adriana asked, "Is there a problem, Mrs. Raines?"

The woman sighed as she looked back toward the gentleman's room and saw the servant once again returning with tray in hand. "His lordship is being difficult about following doctor's orders, miss. However am I to entice him to eat what he ought?"

Adriana eyed the unappetizing meal and knew she couldn't blame his lordship. She bit her lip debating what to do to help, then forged ahead, knowing she might bring the housekeeper's wrath upon her once again. "You may not know this, Mrs. Raines, but I nursed both of my parents for several years in *Roma* before they died. If you don't think I am presuming too much, I have a recipe that might just suit both the doctor's orders and Lord Borland's appetite."

A look of relief flooded the housekeeper's angular features. "I would take any suggestion at the moment, miss."

The two women turned and made for the dining room as Adriana explained a simple recipe given her by an Italian doctor. Mrs. Raines listened carefully to the directions and the ingredients, then smiled. "Why, 'tis so simple yet sounds like it will satisfy his lordship's hunger."

They arrived at the dining room and a footman opened the door. Inside, Adriana could see Lady Underhill and Miss Underhill already seated at the table. Adriana preferred to go to the kitchens instead of facing her dinner companions, but she was no coward. About to enter the dining room, she stopped and said, "Make certain Cook toasts the bread very hard. That is the secret."

"I shall see Cook follows the recipe to the letter, miss." Mrs. Raines gave a nod of her head, then hurried in the direction of the kitchens.

With a wistful sigh, Adriana went in to endure her

supper, wondering what had brought about Mrs. Raines's changed attitude. She might never know, but she was grateful all the same.

Stiffening her back, she said, "Good evening, Lady Underhill, Miss Underhill."

Her ladyship lifted her lorgnette and glared at Adriana. "Is it your usual custom to keep people waiting, Miss Addington? I cannot think the Countess of Wotherford will tolerate such remiss behavior."

Certain that no explanation she could give would satisfy the lady, Adriana merely apologized and took the seat the footman held for her. The meal was as painstakingly dull as she suspected it would be. Lady Underhill dominated the conversation, giving neither her daughter nor Adriana the opportunity to speak. Not that Miss Underhill showed any inclination to do so, spending much of her time inspecting the silver, the dishes, and the glasses as if she expected them to be hers one day.

Halfway through the third remove, a sole in lemon and dill sauce, the dining room door opened and young Nick peeked in. Seeing the object of his search, he threw open the door and came skipping up to Miss Addington. He looked resplendent in claret velvet and silver buttons.

"Look at me, miss. Ain't I fine as five pence in me new uniform?" He put out his arms and turned about.

"What is the meaning of this interruption, boy?" Lady Underhill puffed up like a toad at the sight of a young footman intruding on their meal.

Adriana, hoping to forestall a tongue-lashing by the baroness, rose. "Pray forgive young Nick. He is quite unused to his new position as Lord Borland's personal footman. His lordship kindly saved him from the whip of a harsh master." She heard Miss Underhill gasp, but her mother merely eyed the lad as if it were all a hum.

Pulling Nick along, Adriana headed toward the door. "I shall take him where he belongs. Good night, ladies."

The pair departed the room, Nick looking like he'd lost his best friend. As the door closed behind them, he paused and gazed forlornly at Adriana. "I done wrong comin' in there to see ye, didn't I?"

She ruffled his blond hair. "Don't worry, my boy. I'm certain his lordship won't fault you for a few mistakes when you are learning to be a footman."

At that moment the green baize door to the kitchen opened and Mrs. Raines and the maid, once again carrying a tray, came into the hall. "There you are, Miss Addington. I have his lordship's dinner and I was wondering . . . well, young Bess here is afraid. I hoped . . ."

Adriana smiled. "You hoped that I might be brave enough to take the concoction to the gentleman. I should be delighted."

With obvious relief the maid passed the tray to the young lady, then hurried back in the direction of the kitchens.

"Is Lord Borland usually such a difficult master, Mrs. Raines?"

The lady puckered her brow in thought. "Why, I have never known him to say so much as a harsh word to anyone here, miss. Only this time he seems quite unlike himself."

"No doubt it is his injury that is making him gruff. You needn't worry about sending someone to fetch these things. I shall bring the tray down after the gentleman has eaten and I have read to him as he requested. Come, Nick, I need you to perform an errand for me while I convince Lord Borland this soup is just the thing that will suit him tonight."

Mrs. Raines watched as the young lady and the lad made their way up the main staircase. Things had been quite different since the gentleman awoke, but she wasn't certain it had anything to do with his lordship's injury. Had he at last fallen under the spell of a woman?

The housekeeper realized she'd been wrong to treat Miss Addington as she first had, especially if she wanted to keep her position. She'd done only her duty, as she had so many times before, trying to protect the viscount from marriage-minded females who pursued the gentleman. But it hadn't been until she'd heard his lordship asking the young lady to return to his room and read for him that she realized that unlike Janetta Underhill and her ilk, his lordship actually seemed to like this female. If they were lucky, they might yet be spared Randolph Jamison as master of Borwood Abbey. On that positive thought, the housekeeper went to search out Curtwood and ask his opinion on the matter.

Eight

A knock sounded on Lord Borland's chamber door. The viscount crossed his arms over his chest, quite determined to do battle with Mrs. Raines over the matter of his meal. Had he allowed his housekeeper to fall into the role that his mother had once played, trying to manage his life? He wouldn't tolerate it. He'd been almost a full day without anything other than broth, and he wanted something more substantial. The ache in his head had nearly gone, and he was eager to be up and about. For that he would need a hardy meal.

"Enter," he called.

The door opened and his arms dropped to his sides. Instead of Bess or Mrs. Raines, Miss Addington stepped into the room carrying his tray. Her deep pink gown, while not the height of fashion, suited her dark coloring perfectly as well as her elegant figure. When she smiled at him, something stirred deep in him, and he suddenly didn't care a fig about what was on the tray.

"Good evening, my lord. Mrs. Raines asked me to bring you your supper."

Suddenly Borland returned to his senses at the mention of his housekeeper. He suspected that Mrs. Raines had sent the enchanting young lady to cozen him into accepting something other than what he'd ordered. He scowled at the bowl. "If Mrs. Raines thinks she can turn me up sweet by sending you in here with that pap, she is sadly

mistaken. If I have to climb out of this bed and go to
the kitchens to find something decent, I shall. I won't
eat barley broth and bread tonight, nor any other night
for that matter."

"Nor would I bring such to you, my lord, for fear I
should be wearing it back to the kitchen." Adriana
grinned while she set the tray in front of William, knowing that the aroma would quell his temper better than
anything she might say. She drew back and watched as
he eyed the soup doubtfully, then sniffed the steam rising
from the bowl and looked at her.

"It certainly smells much more enticing. What is it?"
He picked up his spoon and stirred the soup around.

"I fear I have been interfering in your affairs again. I
suggested one of the recipes I brought from Italy as a
replacement to the edible but boring barley broth your
physician ordered. My father's doctor recommended it to
me. It was his mother's recipe. He merely called it *Zuppa
Antonio*. He claimed it was a far better cure than any
medicine he could give."

Hunger spurred the viscount and he tasted the soup.
A smile lit his face. "Excellent—" But before he could
say another word, a knock sounded at the door and Nick
entered without waiting for anyone to call.

" 'Ere's that book ye was wantin', Miss Addington."

"Thank you, Nick. If you should like to listen, find a
place and be quiet."

The viscount eyed the book with interest while Nick
made his way back to the window seat. "What have you
chosen?"

Adriana moved to the chair at the end of the bed. "A
book that comes highly recommended. Eat your dinner
and I shall read to you."

Too hungry to argue about the lady's selection, Borland returned his concentration to the delicious soup the
young lady had brought. It looked nothing like the barley

broth, and one whiff had told him it was not bland and the taste was sheer delight. It wasn't the beefsteak he'd demanded, but the soup was too good to pass up, besides which he was to have a beautiful lady read to him as he ate.

Adriana watched his lordship eat for only a moment, then she opened the book, cleared her throat, and began to read. Her voice was melodic and strong, and she did not hesitate or stumble over the words. Despite her claims of not being a great reader, she had in fact spent many hours doing just that for her invalid mother and dying father.

Having thought himself ravenous, William was surprised when he'd eaten a little over half of the soup and discovered himself feeling satisfied. Perhaps he wasn't as fully recovered as he thought. He pushed the half-eaten meal aside, lay his head on his pillow, closed his eyes, and listened to the dulcet tones of Miss Addington's rich voice. She read exceedingly well, giving unique inflections to the different roles in the story.

Suddenly William's eyes flew open. "Are you reading me a novel, Miss Addington?"

Amber eyes gazed back innocently, but there was a distinct twitch at the corner of the young lady's pink lips. "Why, I am, sir." Then she leaned forward. "I promised my aunt to read these volumes and return them to her in London during the Season. So, I thought since I was planning on reading to you this evening, why, I might kill two birds with one stone, as the old saying goes."

The viscount rolled his eyes. "I think I would prefer you throw those stones at me. I don't think I can abide listening to a silly gothic novel."

"Really, my lord? Are you quite sure you were paying proper attention? 'Tis not a gothic at all. I have read only a few pages, but it seems very amusing to me. The father in the story is delightfully scathing and the mother as dim and determined to wed her daughters as any I've ever seen. Perhaps if I begin again you might see what I mean." She waited a moment, and when the viscount said nothing but only continued to gaze at her, she added, "Or I might leave you alone to rest if you prefer, my lord?"

William suddenly realized he didn't care what the young lady read. He liked hearing her soothing voice. "Pray don't leave. Begin again and I shall pay attention." When the young lady quirked a delicate brow, he grinned. "I promise."

So the young lady started at the beginning of the novel and read for nearly an hour. To the viscount's amazement, he found that despite the occasional distraction of watching Miss Addington play with a dark curl near her ear as she read, he laughed at the author's ability to hold a mirror up to the absurdities of modern society.

At last Adriana closed the book. "That is an excellent stopping place for tonight." She rose and signaled to Nick, who was half asleep on the window seat. "We shall leave you so you might rest."

William rose up on one elbow, nearly toppling the tray that still sat before him. "Thank you. I must own that despite my unkind words about such books, I found your novel very enjoyable. Who is the author? I might purchase some of his other works."

Adriana put the book on William's bedside table and picked up the tray. Nick stood holding the door open as she answered, "Why, as to that I can only say that the story merely says it was 'Written by a Lady.' "

She laughed at the expression on the viscount's face. "Good night, my lord." With that, she departed. After shooing Nick off to bed, she returned the tray to the kitchens, where Mrs. Raines was delighted to see that his lordship had drunk most of the broth. Bidding the lady good night, Adriana went up to bed.

After blowing out her candle for the night, she wondered how long they would stay at Borwood Abbey. That, no doubt, would depend on Dr. Burrell's opinion of Lord Borland's condition. Adriana realized she had quite liked being with the viscount this evening.

A bitterly cold wind arose during the night, freezing the newly fallen snow to a crusty, hard surface. There would be no visitors in or out of Borwood the following day. This news would have been a delight to Lady Underhill's plans but for the fact that the baroness awoke with a frightful cold from all her jaunts back and forth from Hillsborough to Borwood the previous day.

Miss Janetta was summoned to her mother's room and given a list of orders. Foremost, she was to try to manage a visit to his lordship in his sickroom by hook or by crook. Lady Underhill had decided to throw caution to the wind. She was becoming desperate since they lacked the funds to present the pretty Janetta in London and Borland was the last remaining bachelor of good fortune and reputation in the neighborhood. The problem was that the young lady, who owned a remarkably pretty countenance with her sky-blue eyes and guinea-gold curls, had few wits to complement her physical looks.

Miss Underhill's one unfailing characteristic was her absolute determination to follow her mother's orders. She'd learned obedience years earlier after being locked in a linen closet for two days.

Sent on her way by her scheming mama, Janetta stood in the hallway pondering how best to visit the gentleman. Then, with a shrug, she realized it shouldn't be that difficult. She could just walk right into the viscount's room if she merely went up to the door and knocked.

She marched along the corridor of the wing where she and her mother had been relegated and into the main hall, where the master of the house's apartments lay. As she hurried toward her destination, she was surprised to see the little footman who'd barged into the dining room the night before seated beside his lordship's chamber door.

Paying little heed to the lad as she did most servants, she went straight past him and raised her arm to knock on the door. To her amazement and chagrin, the little beast jumped between her and the oak portal. "What ye doin' 'ere, miss?"

"That should be obvious. I've come to pay a visit to Lord Borland. Out of my way, boy."

"No, ye can't. Ain't no one to disturb 'im while 'e's sleepin'. Mrs. Raines's orders." The boy jutted out a stubborn chin as though he intended to do battle if the lady didn't go away.

"Why, I've been at the abbey an entire day and still haven't seen the gentleman. Who are you to be telling me I cannot do what I wish?" She stamped her foot, hoping to frighten the boy into letting her pass.

Nick crossed his arms. "Ye can stomp a 'ole in the floor, miss, and it won't make no difference. I'm 'is lordship's pers—er, perk—I'm his lordship's own footman. Until the gent 'imself tells me or Mrs. Raines says, ain't nobody goin' in that room today."

In a rage, Janetta huffed off down the hall. This wasn't going to be as easy as she'd first thought. As she stormed down the passageway, her first thought was to return to report to her mother, then she realized that she would merely be sent to try again. She would show her mother she could handle matters well enough on her own.

Once she rounded the corner and was out of sight of Borland's little red-coated watchdog, she began to put her mind to the task of how she might gain entry into Lord Borland's room. No doubt his chamber was very much like her late father's. She bit her lip and wrinkled her brow at the effort of so much thought.

Then she remembered she'd always snuck in to wake her father through his dressing room. She eyed the door behind her and wondered if there might not be a similar connecting door to his lordship's rooms.

The chamber door was unlocked and Janetta entered, but she soon discovered that while the room did have such a door, it proved to be on the opposite side from his lordship's room. She would have to think of something else.

About to leave, her gaze stopped at a set of doors that led out onto a small balcony. She hurried across the room and opened the door, remembering that at Hillsborough all the balconies connected.

Cold air penetrated her thin pink muslin gown. Shivering, she poked her head out just long enough to see that the two balconies didn't join, but there was a wide ledge that ran from one to the other. Janetta slammed the doors shut and drew back into the room as she rubbed her arms to stop the chills.

Still cold, she began to pace back and forth as she considered her options. Clearly, that little brat of a footman wasn't going to let her in. That left the balcony as the only other portal to the gentleman. Dare she attempt to walk that ledge? She peered out one more time. Ivy clung thickly to the side of the building. She could hold onto those tangled vines and make her way over to his balcony. Then she looked at the ground below and she shivered but not from the cold. It was a long way down. About to abandon her foolhardy plan, she remembered that dreaded linen closet at Hillsborough and knew she was more afraid of her mother than of what might happen should she fall.

With a plan set, Janetta realized she couldn't go without a coat or something warmer or she would freeze halfway across. She exited the room, hurrying by his lordship's chamber. She couldn't resist a glance at the door. Then her gaze dropped to the boy whose green eyes were narrowed.

"Don't be thinkin' 'bout goin' in this room."

Janetta stuck out her tongue, then hurried down the hall as the lad whistled and hooted softly at her childish behavior.

In her room she had no choice in wraps, having been unable to pack properly for their rushed visit to Borwood. That would have been suspicious to his lordship's servants. She donned the black velvet spencer she'd worn the day before, then hurried back into the main hall. Without so much as a word or a look, she sailed past the feisty little footman. She rounded the corner of the hall and ducked back into the room she'd entered before.

Nick, while quite young, was no fool. He was certain that the pretty girl with the bad temper was up to something. She'd pranced back and forth in front of him like a grand horse on parade. Was she still trying to force her way in to see Lord Borland?

Curious what she was about, Nick tiptoed down the hall and peered around the corner. There was not a soul in sight and all the doors were closed. He straightened and scratched his head. He'd roved the abbey a great deal over the past day and a half, and he thought this hall was a dead end. Something just wasn't right. He suddenly decided that he must go and find Miss Addington. She would know what to do about that sneaking female. He didn't want to be in trouble for anything that nosy miss might do.

Not wanting to be away from his post long, Nick raced down the hall. At the young lady's chamber he found only Nancy, cleaning the room. The maid informed him that Miss Addington had gone down to breakfast. Nick dashed back to his lordship's door to make certain that the girl hadn't returned. Seeing nothing suspicious, he rushed to the hallway where she'd disappeared, and saw nothing. With things quiet, he ran full tilt to find Miss Addington.

The young lady was enjoying her breakfast in solitude when the door burst open and a breathless Nick dashed in. "Miss, I think somethin' "—the lad had to stop to gasp before he continued—" 'avey-cavey is goin' on upstairs."

Adriana picked up a pitcher and poured the boy a glass of water. "Calm down and tell me whatever do you mean."

The lad emptied the glass, then said, "That mort with the yellow 'air's tryin' to enter 'is lordship's room, even though I done told 'er the gent ain't receivin' whilst 'e's ailin'."

"Do you mean Miss—" A piercing scream interrupted Adriana. The sound wasn't a hurried shout but a shrill call that seemed to go on forever. She realized at once it came from just outside the breakfast parlor window. She dashed to the arched portal, throwing it open.

To her amazement, Adriana discovered Miss Janetta Underhill hanging upside down, or who one must assume to be the girl, for her head was covered with yards of pink muslin and white petticoats, exposing lacy pantaloons, stockings, and garters. One pink-slippered foot was tangled in the thick ivy vines on the second floor and was all that kept her from falling to the ground. Janetta looked very much like the wilted bloom of a spring flower with her skirts over her head.

"What ye doin' up there?" Nick blurted out as he poked his head out the window beside Adriana.

"Trying to fly away from this cursed place, you little beast. Now go away to fetch some help and stop asking utterly stupid questions." With that, the girl fruitlessly tried to push her gown up to cover her exposed limbs.

When her attempt proved useless, she once again began to wail.

Nick shook his head as he eyed the sight. "The lady ain't got bird wings, but she's sure got a bird's brain in 'er box if she thinks she can fly."

Adriana was puzzled herself at the girl's odd situation, but merely called, "Miss Underhill, you must not wiggle about so or your foot will come free and you will fall to the ground." To Nick she said, "Find Mrs. Raines! She must send footmen to the south portico immediately. They will need ladders."

Nick shook his head as he drew back from the window. "I knew 'er was up to no good."

Adriana again leaned out to calm the softly wailing girl. "Stay very still, Miss Underhill. We shall have help there in a matter of minutes."

But before Adriana could move, a balcony door to the left of where the young lady was hanging opened and Lord Borland appeared in a blue brocade dressing gown. A stunned expression settled on his handsome face as he spied the dangling female. Then his gaze moved to Adriana's upturned face. "What is going on here, Miss Addington?"

"Miss Underhill has taken a tumble, my lord. I have sent Nick for help. Pray do not worry. The servants shall have her safely down in a moment." Adriana hoped he didn't ask where the girl had fallen from since she couldn't provide a reasonable explanation.

A scowl settled on William's face as his gaze swept the side of the building. He quickly noted the open balcony door across the way. It was evident at once what Miss Underhill had been about from her position between the two rooms. Of all the crackbrained ideas to try and walk the ledge to his room.

William swore under his breath. Miss Addington might say he was foolish to think all women were silly and ambitious, but once again he had evidence to the contrary.

Within minutes a small army of footmen, curious maids, and Mrs. Raines hurried out of the south portico. They trudged through the snow to peer at the stranded Miss Underhill. There was a stunned moment when all halted at the sight of the lady who appeared all legs and petticoats. When one of the maids tittered, the housekeeper seemed to remember her duty and shouted, "Don't stand around gaping like monkeys, help the young lady down."

Ladders were braced on either side of her. The two largest footmen climbed up and quickly untangled the lady's foot, then lowered her to waiting hands. By the time Miss Underhill was turned right side up, her gown properly about her ankles, she was little more than a whimpering, red-faced, quivering lump, quite unable to walk. Even Mrs. Raines exhibited a bit of sympathy for the chit and ordered a footman and maid to see her safely to her rooms.

As Adriana watched them lead the girl away, it became clear that the young lady had meant to reach Lord Borland's rooms, but for what purpose one could only imagine.

At that thought, Adriana looked up to his lordship's balcony, but Borland had returned indoors without a word. Still, his annoyed expression had spoken volumes. There had been such a look of disgust on the viscount's countenance, Adriana had it in her heart to pity Miss Underhill. She was thankful the girl's face had been so obscured by her skirts, she hadn't seen the viscount's reaction to her foolish stunt.

Drawing back and closing the window, Adriana felt sympathy for Lord Borland also. She realized life for a wealthy titled gentleman must never be easy when there were marriage-minded females determined to go to such lengths to snare them. No wonder the viscount was so standoffish and contemptuous of females. No doubt he'd seen little to make him think well of her gender.

Nick brought Adriana out of her reverie by quickly bidding her good-bye, saying he must return to his post. Once again alone, she sat down to finish her meal, but it had grown quite cold. Pushing her plate aside, her thoughts returned to the distaste evident on Lord Borland's face as he'd stared down at a topsy-turvy Janetta Underhill. Adriana hoped she never gave him cause to look at her with such contempt.

The viscount closed the balcony door, then stood for a moment staring into the distant snow-covered fields. This newest episode with Miss Underhill had brought back all his feelings of abhorrence for the idea of a female residing in his household. All women did was cause disruption and put the servants to a great deal of bother only to gain their own wishes.

Standing there, the viscount suddenly remembered the reason Miss Addington had been foisted on him—his grandmother and her damnable plotting to make him marry. True, Miss Addington hadn't pursued him, but, female that she was, she had created one disturbance after another, gathering a veritable legion of misfits as they'd traveled along. He needed to remember that the next time he found himself admiring the arch of her neck or the twinkle in those amazing amber eyes.

Furious that he'd allowed himself to be drawn to a young lady sent by Lady Margaret in her never-ending matchmaking, William promised himself not to fall prey to a pair of laughing brown eyes and tantalizing lips. When he'd started this journey he had been content with his life. And nothing had changed. Or so he told himself. With a dismissive shrug of his shoulders, he turned and strode to the fireplace. Settling in front of the flames, he decided that until Dr. Burrell gave him a clean bill of health, he'd best avoid Adriana.

If the tales about his cousin were true, and young Katy seemed evidence that they were, he might yet be forced to take a wife. And if he must, the lady should be one who was quiet, scholarly, and reserved, not some madcap chit without the least interest in his studious way of life.

Some two days later *The Post* was once again delivered to Borwood Abbey, alerting the residents that the roads were at last open. For Adriana's part, she was delighted. It meant they might be able to leave for Scotland as soon as the doctor arrived and informed them of the viscount's health. She'd found herself quite isolated since Miss Underhill's accident. Lord Borland had not only ceased to request her presence for some odd reason, leaving her feeling decidedly unhappy, but had left orders with Nick to bar her from his room.

Not wanting to dwell on her disappointment, she'd realized that she had no Christmas gift to give Lady Margaret and decided to do a drawing of Lord Borland. When she started the sketch, she was amazed at how well she knew his every feature, but then, after all, she was an artist. Yet, except for the sketch of the highwayman, this was her first portrait without having the model in front of her. Still, her hand moved boldly over the paper. The drawing kept her nicely occupied in her solitude.

Miss Underhill had stayed sequestered in her room since her unfortunate fall, as had her mother in hers. That morning, upon being told the roads were once again passable, the young lady rose with a newly developed determination and dressed, then forced her protesting mother to do the same. What Janetta told Lady Underhill of her accident, no one knew, but that lady looked positively defeated as she came downstairs with her daughter, requiring the supporting arms of two maids. It was uncertain if her sniffles were due to her lost hopes or her cold.

The ladies quietly boarded their hastily summoned coach after sending their compliments to the viscount along with wishes for a speedy recovery. Without a backward glance they set off for Hillsborough.

His lordship's uninvited guests had scarcely been gone twenty minutes when Dr. Burrell arrived and went straight up to the viscount. Adriana eagerly awaited news of Lord Borland's health in the breakfast parlor, knowing the physician would soon be down and looking for sustenance.

When the doctor entered the room, his gaze riveted on the tray of warm cinnamon buns just delivered by a footman. Adriana rose, saying, "How is his lordship?" In truth she feared that her exclusion from the sickroom had been due to William's having taken a turn for the worse. Nick had tried to assure her that the viscount was in prime twig despite sequestering himself in his room, but still, doubts lingered.

The doctor settled himself at the table and poured a cup of coffee. "Why, he's back to his old self, as best I can tell. Reading a book, he was, when I entered his room. It was quite like old times, save he wasn't in his library. But that shall soon be remedied, for he intends coming down later." With that, he took a large bite of a sticky bun.

Adriana wasn't sure that "being his old self" was such good news. Did that mean he was once again the starched, unfriendly gentleman she'd met in London only a few days before?

But before she could ask any further questions, the doctor swallowed, then added, "That doesn't mean I think he should continue his journey to Scotland as yet. I'm afraid all that rattling about on the road might bring on the headache again if he doesn't take care for a few more days. He needs to be up and about here at the abbey to regain his strength before such a journey. Told him you could still make her ladyship's Christmas party in plenty of time if you leave by the end of the week."

Loud voices echoed in the hallway, causing the doctor to turn and listen. "Good thing he's ready to receive visitors. My guess is much of the neighborhood is eager to come and hear all the details of the robbery."

Adriana arched one brow. "But his lordship still has no memory of the event." Or at least he hadn't the last time she'd spoken to him.

"Likely he never will, but young Nick tells me the lot of you have filled Borland's memory gap nicely, so he'll be able to spin a yarn for the gossips, who will be eager for all the lurid details, if he should choose to do such."

Curious when she would see the viscount again, Adriana bid the doctor good morning. She decided to go to her room and put the finishing touches on her portrait of the gentleman. She'd barely gone halfway up the stairs, when Lord Borland appeared at the top, dressed in a morning coat of dark blue over a waistcoat of gray. His bandage now gone, his sandy-brown hair was combed neatly around his handsome face, leaving no evidence of his injury.

"Good morning, my lord." Adriana smiled to see him looking so much like his former self. "I hope you are feeling much better."

There was no answering smile. Lord Borland gave a slight formal nod to her at her greeting, then coolly replied, "I am much recovered, Miss Addington." Without further comment he swept past her.

Adriana turned and watched as he disappeared into what she assumed was his library, her heart sinking. Whatever had brought about the return of his unfriendly demeanor? Was this all about Miss Underhill's foolish stunt? Adriana wanted him to be as he had been when she'd read to him, friendly and questioning. He'd been so handsome, even with his head bound, watching her so intently. Even now her heart fluttered at the memory of those blue eyes fixed on her each time she'd looked up from the book she'd read. She sighed. Clearly, she was not to see that side of Lord Borland again.

Never one to dwell on dark matters, she decided that perhaps with a little time he might return to a lighter, friendlier mood. With a shrug of her shoulders, Adriana realized there was little she could do about him now. If he was determined to think all women were cut from the same cloth, what did it matter to her? Nancy said they were only a little over a day's journey from Wother Castle, which meant she was not likely to spend much time in his lordship's company again. On that surprisingly daunting thought, she went to her room.

The doctor's prophecy proved correct. Over the course of the morning a steady stream of his lordship's curious neighbors arrived to hear the tale of the highwaymen firsthand, although most left with no added information. Adriana got no chance to speak with the viscount again.

There was very much a part of her that wanted the gentleman to summon her, but no such call came. For the time being he seemed quite determined to dislike her once again—because of his grandmother forcing him to escort her or Miss Underhill's unfortunate accident, Adriana didn't know which.

Determined to put the matter from her mind, she set out to find Signora, who'd gone missing all morning. She learned from Mrs. Raines that the cat had last been seen making her way through the snow toward the stables. Adriana went to her room and donned her bonnet, woolen cape, and walking boots, then went in search of the animal. She suspected that the feline was about to deliver her litter any day and didn't want the newborn kittens to be out in the cold.

A path had been shoveled from the rear of the house to the stables. The remaining bits of snow and ice crunched under Adriana's boots as she made her way from the abbey. At the crest of a small rise, she stood a moment savoring the warmth of the sun on her face as she looked around. At last, on reaching the large stone building she peered in, but the grooms all seemed much too busy to disturb. Hesitant to be in their way, she turned to look back at Borwood Abbey and got her first good view of its exterior. It was a long, sprawling building of gray stone and arched windows, the symmetrical square-cut roof running the length of the structure. She couldn't see the entire abbey due to the tall sculpted yews that bordered the rear gardens. She wished she could walk around and examine the wonderful old structure from every angle, even do a drawing, but the snow was too deep for such exploration.

A shout echoed on the cold morning air. Nick ran toward her along the same cleared path she'd taken. "Miss Addington, Miss Addington!"

She waved and smiled, but there was no answering smile on the child's face. Suddenly she wondered if his lordship had suffered a relapse from leaving the sickroom too early.

The boy slid to a stop on the icy walk, then gasped, "Ye must come at once."

She grabbed the lad to steady him, saying, "Be careful or you will take a tumble on the ice, Nick."

But the boy was too excited. "Never mind about that, miss. Ye must come with me at once. 'Tis important."

"Very well, but what is this about? Is his lordship ill? Or have you found Signora?"

Nick tugged on her arm, impatient with her reluctance to act. "Come with me. I'll show ye."

Adriana allowed herself to be pulled along the path back to the abbey, deciding to let the boy show her this mysterious thing, for he was greatly agitated.

She began to have second thoughts about what she was doing as they ran out of cleared pathway and had to forge through the deeper snow along the edge of the house. Had Nick gotten into some great mischief and hoped she might calm the housekeeper's ire?

They came to what appeared to be a wall of shrubbery, trimmed to a tall hedge. Nick raised his hand. "Wait 'ere, miss." He then disappeared into a hole in the greenery. Within minutes he returned, a satisfied expression on his face. "Go in 'ere, ye can see what it is that I want ye to see."

Adriana eyed the entry into the shrubs doubtfully, then shrugged. What did it matter? She would nip in, take a look, and be out in a matter of minutes. She pushed the branches aside and squeezed into the tight space that Nick had gone through easily. The limbs inside the hedge tugged at her bonnet, pulling it from her head, then began to work their destruction on her neatly coiled black curls. She would look a fright once she exited the foliage, but she had started this little adventure and would see it through for Nick's sake.

Inside the gap in the hedge, Adriana halted just before she could have stepped into the light on the other side. What she could see was a beautiful snow-covered garden completely enclosed by the dense evergreen hedge in which she stood. A white marble statue of Pegasus stood at one end, front hooves reared in the air, its white tail and mane appearing to flow in the wind as the mythical animal looked about to take flight. The pristine snow gave the small area a magical look, as if only fairies lived there. While it was very beautiful, she couldn't imagine this being what had gotten Nick so excited. He was only a child and thus far had shown little interest in nature's wonders.

As Adriana looked around, it appeared the only access to the private sanctuary would be through the doors from the abbey. The doors in question led to Lord Borland's library. Was this a private garden where his lordship could come to read in peace?

In truth, she'd done little inspecting of the abbey and hadn't been inside that room. From her vantage point in the shrubbery, she could see through the tall windows. The room appeared just as she would have expected a scholarly man's library to look. Stacks of books cluttered the tables; floor-to-ceiling bookshelves overflowed. There was even an upper catwalk to gain access to the books near the high ceiling. Then a movement caught her eye.

Two gentlemen stood laughing and talking before what appeared to be the box of books Lord Borland had brought from London. His lordship's smile warmed her heart. Surely his mood was much improved from when she'd encountered him on the stairs. She suddenly felt like an intruder, peering in at the gentlemen in this fashion.

She was about to turn and leave, when his lordship handed his visitor a book and that gentleman, who had been facing away from the windows, turned to read the cover, giving her a full look at his face.

Adriana gasped and knew at once why Nick had brought her to this hedge. She found herself looking into the same villainous face she had seen only days before.

The highwayman stood in Lord Borland's library.

Nine

Adriana's mind whirled. She must do something, but she didn't know what. Should she confront the highwayman or wait until after he left and inform his lordship? She turned and pushed her way out of the tight hedge, too upset this time to take note of the pricks and pulls of the tiny branches. When she stepped out on the far side, Nick's eyes widened at the sight of her. The limbs had tugged a cascade of curls loose from her topknot, and she had a tiny scratch on her cheek and a rip in the sleeve of her gown.

"Are ye all right, miss?"

Oblivious of her disheveled condition, she said, "It is the highwayman. We must do something."

"Don't want 'im to escape, that's fer sure. Got to tell 'is lordship at once."

But Adriana wasn't so certain. Would the viscount believe that this man had stopped their coach and robbed them? That a friend could strike him down in such a manner and even try to shoot Nick? Then her memory stuck on a fact she'd paid little heed to during the actual event. The highwayman had known Lord Borland, for he'd referred to him as "his lordship."

Friend or foe, decisive action was called for at that very moment. "Go tell Thomas to summon the constable, Nick."

As the child dashed back through the snow, Adriana

hurried to the door she'd exited the abbey by and made her way up to her room. She pulled open a drawer in a Sheraton chest and drew out her small pistol.

As if to give herself courage in what she was about to do, she spoke out loud. "I shall detain him until the constable can arrive."

Adriana left her chamber without so much as a glance in the cheval glass, still unaware of her frightful appearance. She made her way down the main staircase. Upon reaching the library door, she hesitated just long enough to hide the pistol under the edge of her woolen cape. Perhaps had she given herself time to think about this impromptu plan, she wouldn't have proceeded. At present she was running on a wave of outrage and anger that a gentleman could be such a scoundrel, so without even a knock she marched into the library.

The gentlemen had moved to a pair of matched brown leather wing chairs in front of the fireplace. Upon hearing the door open, they both looked in her direction and started from their seats, surprise on his lordship's face and amusement on the villain's.

"Good God, Miss Addington, what have you been about now?" Lord Borland admonished. "You look as if you have been pulled through a hedgerow backward."

In a feminine gesture, Adriana's unencumbered hand went to her hair. She must look a fright, but for the moment she regarded her appearance as unimportant. "Actually I was in the shrubbery."

His lordship's visitor held up a quizzing glass and peered at the young lady, spying a twig in her disheveled raven locks. "I think she means that literally. Out communing with the local wildlife perchance, or does she imagine herself a sparrow? Nay, she is too tall for such a tiny bird, I think more likely a gray heron. Whichever, I am delighted to see you have such an interesting guest, old friend."

Adriana's amber gaze blazed with anger. "How can you call him that, sir, after what you have done?"

The viscount's countenance grew grim at her insult. "Miss Addington, what new piece of work is this? How dare you insult Sir Perrick Kingston."

"Sir Perrick, indeed!" Adriana knew what was before her eyes. This was the man who had robbed them on the road. Nick had known it the moment he'd seen him and so had she. "My lord, your friend has a dark secret. Do you wish to tell him, Sir Perrick, or shall I?"

The baronet dropped his quizzing glass and grinned as he glanced from the glowering young lady to his outraged friend. "I am all agog, waiting to hear this secret. I thought my scandals were an open book to all of London. 'Tis truly a delight to find there is one secret left that ain't common knowledge. But, Will, you must introduce me to your delightfully amusing houseguest. Or should I simply call her Lady Heron? Cannot keep all this loveliness to yourself."

The viscount wasn't certain who he was more exasperated with, Miss Addington and her strange insults or Perry for his incessant flirting. Still, William performed the introductions. This newest start of accusing one of his friends of dark doings was the worst yet of the young lady's many antics.

"Perry, allow me to present Miss Adriana Addington, my grandmother's new companion. Miss Addington, Sir Perrick Kingston of Kingston Lodge."

The baronet moved forward, intending to take the lady's hand gallantly, but he froze when from beneath her cape a small pistol appeared.

"Stay where you are, sir."

Despite the danger, the gentleman merely grinned and returned to Lord Borland's side. "I cannot own many principles in my dissipated life, but never argue with a woman holding a pistol has always been one rule I live by, truly."

Before Borland could comment, the door to the library burst open and Nick appeared. He hurried to Adriana's side. "Thomas is gone to fetch the law, miss."

The viscount had had enough of this farce. "Miss Addington, I demand that you put down that gun at once before—"

Adriana's chin rose. "I am quite capable of handling a firearm, my lord."

Sir Perry eyed the weapon as he moved toward the desk where his riding crop lay. "I am still uncertain what this dark secret is of which you are accusing me, Miss Addington." He picked up the small whip, measuring the distance between him and the young lady. He suspected he might strike the weapon from her at any time if he were closer.

Nick's eyes narrowed as the man moved to within feet of the young lady. "Shoot 'im if 'e comes too close, miss. 'E's got eyes like a rat."

Sir Perrick straightened. "Surely not a rat. I refute the idea of having anything like a rodent. How about a fox's eyes?" The gentleman eyed the boy hopefully but got only a scowl in return.

William feared that between them, Miss Addington and Nick would do Perry a serious injury. The viscount moved forward, stepping between the lady and the baronet. "Give me that gun at once, then explain this outrage."

Looking into the gentleman's eyes, Adriana again saw that steely determination to be obeyed in the viscount's gaze. His glowering intensity seemed to sap her will. She lowered the pistol, then allowed Lord Borland to take it from her. When Borland, gun in hand, moved to stand once again at Kingston's side, Adriana tried to explain.

"My lord, your friend is leading a double life. Nick

and I saw his face when he was unmasked at the robbery. Sir Perrick Kingston is a highwayman."

The viscount and the baronet turned to gaze at each other in stunned surprise. Then they both burst into laughter, leaving Adriana to think Lord Borland's brains might still be unsettled from the accident. Seeing genuine mirth twinkling in Sir Perry's hazel eyes, she suddenly had the feeling that she was about to learn something that was going to make her actions of the last moments seem very foolish.

After a good laugh and taking note of Miss Addington's still-doubtful countenance, the viscount wiped the smile from his face. "Pray forgive our amusement, but this is not the first time Perry has been falsely accused of a crime. Although this, perhaps, is the first time he's been threatened at gunpoint."

That said, the baronet sobered as well. " 'Tis, indeed. But, Will, allow me to explain this delicate matter to the young lady and your bloodthirsty little footman. My father, Miss Addington, like all Kingston men, fancied the ladies. Unfortunately, he wasn't particular which ones, hence I have several . . . er, low relations in these parts who bear a remarkable resemblance to me, if you understand my meaning. In truth, there is one fellow in Sheffield who could be my twin, which I believe may have been your highwayman, for try as I will to help him better himself, he seems drawn to bad ways."

Adriana stood in appalled silence. She'd actually pointed a pistol at a gentleman, not the brigand she'd suspected. "Oh, Sir Perrick, I must apologize for—"

The baronet gestured her to silence, then moved toward her. Taking one of her hands, he pressed a kiss to it as he gazed into her eyes. "Do not worry yourself over such a trifle. There have been many women who wished to put a hole in me over the years. That's why I find it necessary to have the rule about not arguing with ladies with pistols." Seeing the look of surprise in the young lady's eyes, he grinned. "Miss Addington, allow me to be the one to apologize for Jack Kent's conduct. I fully intend to see that he pays for what he did. Tell me, did the blackguard take anything of value from you?"

The viscount, watching his old friend charm the lady who'd almost shot him, realized that Miss Addington appeared quite incapable of speech at the moment. Was it quite so easy to sweep her off her feet with pretty words, or was she merely mortified at her conduct?

"He did, Perry," William answered, "a keepsake her brother gave her. A gold necklace with Minerva etched on the front and Latin on the back. Do you think you might recover it for her?"

Gallantly, Sir Perrick again raised Adriana's hand and placed a lingering kiss upon it. "For you, lovely lady, I shall track down the villain this very night and find your property."

A little dazed by the gesture, Adriana suddenly remembered that Nick had told Thomas to summon the constable to arrest this man. What a fright that would be should the man come only to discover her foolish mistake.

"That would be most kind, sir. Pray excuse me, but there is an urgent matter I must handle at once." With that Adriana turned on her heel, dragging Nick with her, and dashed out the door.

The baronet chuckled, then eyed his friend. "Quite a beauty your grandmother has employed."

Borland shook his head. "Do you never think of anything else, man? The woman accused you of being a highwayman and nearly shot you." With that, the viscount held up the small pistol he'd taken from Adriana.

"And what does that have to say about her beauty? I may not argue with an armed woman, but, by Jove, I do admire her spirit."

"Spirit, ha! I call it meddling." The viscount moved to his desk to put the gun in the top drawer.

Perry watched his friend, shaking his head. "My dear fellow, your idea of the perfect woman is some little mouse that sits in the corner awaiting your pleasure like some boring tome. When you've had half as many females as I, you will know that the spirited ones like Miss Addington keep life interesting. Why, I've a mind to invite myself along to your grandmother's. 'Twould make for a very amusing Christmas party."

William didn't know why, but the idea of a rake like Perry trifling with an innocent like Adriana made all his goodwill for his friend flee. He snapped, "Go find your dastardly half brother and set things right for the lady. I think she values that necklace a great deal. That will be all the attention a delicately bred female needs from you."

The baronet grinned. "So, I begin to see how matters stand. In truth, I'm delighted for you. As with most others, I'd given up hope."

"What are you gabbling about?"

Sir Perrick picked up his gloves and ignored the viscount's question. "I have a mission to fulfill for your beautiful houseguest. Tell the delightful Miss Addington I shall return with her necklace before you leave for Scotland." Then he paused with a wicked twinkle in his eye to add, "Or if I cannot run Jack to ground so quickly, I perhaps may follow you to Wother Castle."

William had no time to protest such a plan, for his friend strolled out of the library bent on his mission. Had Kingston been implying that the viscount had a tendre for Miss Addington simply because he'd warned him away from the girl? That was ridiculous. He just knew Perry's reputation with women too well.

But the viscount could no longer deny that he was attracted to the lady. Still, he was determined not to let things go any further than attraction. Hadn't she just given him proof of her volatile nature? Keeping her out of trouble would be a full-time job for some man, but not him.

On that final thought, he went to the box of books he'd brought from London and began unloading them, for he never allowed his staff to handle his treasures. Burrell had told him to take it easy for a few days, and that was what he intended to do—if Miss Addington could keep herself out of trouble for so brief a time.

That evening Adriana stepped into the drawing room, her stomach in a bit of a flutter. She was uncertain if the unsettled feeling was due to what sort of reception she would receive by his lordship after her faux pas with his friend, or from being alone once again in the viscount's company after being barred from his presence for two days.

Lord Borland stood tall and handsome in front of the fireplace in his black coat and white waistcoat. He appeared lost in thought as he gazed down into the fire. She was uncertain what had brought on the change in the past two days, but he held much of the stern look she remembered from London. Had the incident in the library caused him to permanently revert to his former behavior? Was he never again to relax and treat her as a friend? She hoped not.

"Good evening, my lord. I hope I'm not disturbing you."

William looked up to see the woman who had interrupted his thoughts far too much. Despite her antics in the library, he still found himself undeniably attracted to her. He noted she wore the same rose gown of the other evening, but she'd added a pale pink cashmere shawl on this occasion. He thought she looked beautiful but a bit pensive. "I was awaiting you. Do come to the fire, Miss Addington, for the abbey is always frightfully chilled in winter."

She moved to stand in front of him. He watched as she appeared to be searching her mind for something to say. She bit at her lip, then looked at him with trepidation.

"I must apologize again for that monstrous mistake with your friend, Sir Perrick, but when Nick saw him and the uncanny resemblance to the highwayman, he came to me and—"

"And your impetuous mind immediately thought to rush headlong for your pistol." He smiled, taking some of the sting out of his words.

She gave a half-laugh even as her gaze never left his face. "I suppose it seemed rather rash, but—"

"Ah, Miss Addington, I suspect there is little chance you will change your nature. I shall only say that on this occasion there was no harm done. Don't give it any more thought. Unfortunately, as long as Jack is on the loose, Perry is in danger of being misidentified again. I've tried to tell him for years to send the man to America, but Perry has always felt an obligation to the villain." The viscount was quiet a moment, then remembering his friend's clear interest in the young lady he thought to give her a warning. "About Perry, I would advise caution with your dealings with him."

Adriana's mouth tipped into a half-smile. "Does a propensity for wickedness run in the Kingston family?"

William was quick to deny such. "Not wickedness. There isn't a better fellow than Perry as a friend. And while he rarely comes to the neighborhood these days, he employs an excellent fellow to manage his land and tenants. Yet, from what I hear, he seems drawn to scandal where women are concerned, much like his father before him."

Adriana arched one dark brow. "Is your friend a rake? I have never met a true rake before."

The viscount shrugged. " 'Tis not for me to say other than to tell you he has broken many a heart. My grandmother says wise mothers keep their daughters away from him."

Tugging her shawl up her shoulders against the room's chill, Adriana made no comment, but the viscount had redirected her thoughts. "About your grandmother, my lord. Do you think she truly has need of a companion?"

Borland was silent a moment, debating what to say. He very much doubted the active old lady wished a companion other than the bevy of loyal retainers who'd surrounded her since Lord Wotherford had died. The countess had lured Miss Addington on this trip with the offer of employment, but he questioned whether his grandmother's plans included the young lady arriving to actually take up the position.

Realizing that Miss Addington required employment due to her straitened circumstances, he decided not to dash her hopes. He suspected the countess would swallow her disappointment when her ploy came to nothing and accept the young lady into her household. "I think my grandmother has been in need of a companion these last five years." Noting Adriana's fingers fidgeting with the fringe on her shawl, William asked, "Are you fearful she will be displeased with you in some way?"

Her amber gaze flew to meet his, and for a moment the breath seemed to catch in William's lungs. She appeared so vulnerable at that moment, he wanted to crush her to him and wipe away all her worries about the future. He forced his gaze to the fire. This young lady seemed to be bewitching him. He almost laughed out loud when he thought of Miss Addington needing a protector. He'd never known a female who needed someone to look after her less than this spirited lady.

At last the troubled miss spoke. "You have been in my company these last few days, my lord. Does it strike you that I shall be a suitable companion for an elderly lady?"

William gave an ironic laugh as he watched the golden flames dance. "Why, I couldn't have chosen a better companion for the countess had I done the interviewing myself. My grandmother is an original, Miss Addington, as you are. I think you will deal famously together."

Adriana hoped he was correct, but she still held doubts. After the incident in the library she'd come to wonder if she was the right person to be a companion. Perhaps she'd managed her family's affairs too long to be docile and subservient enough. She gave a sigh, then realized if things didn't go well with the countess, she could always join her brother at his current station in France, now that there was peace.

Determined not to dwell on the future, she changed the subject once again to inquire of his lordship's health. Assured that he was very much on the mend, the topic moved to the weather and when they would be able to travel, but for the moment Lord Borland thought no decision should be made on any definite plans. They must take things one day at a time.

After some moments the conversation became less stilted and they soon were again discussing topics that interested them both. They spent an enjoyable evening in each other's company, and as Adriana was retiring for the night, she suddenly wished she didn't have to go on to the uncertainty of Scotland.

The changeable English weather brought rain once again to Yorkshire and began the process of removing the remains of the snowstorm. Adriana had scarcely finished dressing, when a footman arrived at her chamber door to announce that Sir Perrick was below in the Willow Drawing Room, awaiting her.

She jumped to her feet after the maid put the last pin in to hold her dark hair in a simple topknot. A few loose curls dangled behind her head. "Oh, Nancy, I do hope the gentleman has found my necklace. I delayed writing to Amy that it was stolen, hoping some miracle would occur and it should again be in my possession."

She dashed toward the door, but the maid called, "Should I not come with you, miss? Ain't proper to be closeted with a gentleman alone."

Adriana laughed. "Don't worry about me, Nancy. I am certain Lord Borland will be there as well. You might do me a favor and see if you can find Signora. She has been missing since yesterday."

Excitement pulsed in Adriana's veins at the hope of recovering her good luck charm, causing her to dash down the hall at an unladylike pace. Upon entering the Willow Drawing Room, she checked upon the threshold.

Sir Perrick stood gazing out at the chilled rain pattering on the windows. Lord Borland was nowhere in sight. Her mind returned to the viscount's warning. This gentleman was an infamous rake, or so his lordship believed. The baronet turned and smiled at her. She took note of his fashionable attire, which included a high collar encircled by a starched cravat with an intricate knot and a brown coat over a tan striped waistcoat. He was handsome to the point of being almost pretty. Long dark lashes framed his hazel eyes and his reddish-blond hair was combed in a windswept fashion about his sculpted face.

Yet, she decided there was little danger of her losing her heart to him. True, he had been charming and very forgiving of her blunder, but she wondered if there was little substance to him other than his charm. In her mind, the very fact that he toyed with the affections of women put a black mark in his books. Clearly, he was not at all like Lord Borland.

That thought startled her. Why would she wish a gentleman to be like the bookish viscount? She pushed aside the worrisome notion and advanced into the room.

"Good morning, Sir Perrick."

"Ah, Miss Addington, you are a feast for my ratlike eyes this cold, wet morning."

Adriana laughed. "I do believe you have the right of it and they have more the cunning look of a fox."

"You greatly relieve my mind."

When the baronet drew her hand to his lips, Adriana felt as if she were a puppet in a play, enacting a performance that had been repeated over and over. This was a man who played a role with women. She tugged her hand free from the lingering grasp. "Have you any news of Mr. Kent?"

Sir Perry scrutinized her for a moment, seeing her almost as a challenge, then thought better of it. He was something of a rogue with the ladies, but his honor would never allow him to do his friend such a turn. That made the lady, no matter how beautiful or disinterested—the more intriguing of the traits—out of bounds.

"That I have, Miss Addington." Perry reached into his pocket and pulled out a small jeweler's box. A frown marred his looks as he watched Adriana tentatively open the box and push the paper aside. "I fear I was unable to recover any of the money taken from the others. I think most of the blunt was wasted on gin, but your necklace was still in his coat pocket. I discovered the chain was broken, no doubt when it was taken, so I took the liberty of replacing it with another."

Adriana lifted the necklace from the silver paper and suddenly choked up, remembering the day Alexander had given it to her. In her gratitude at having recovered the keepsake, she threw her arms around Sir Perrick's neck and stood on tiptoe to kiss his cheek. "Thank you, sir. While it has little real worth, you cannot know the sentimental value this has for me. The last day I saw my brother, he gave it to me. That was almost eight years ago."

The baronet slipped his arms around her waist as naturally as breathing and hugged her back. He decided if Will didn't develop cold feet or become distracted by some dusty tome, he would be a very luck fellow indeed.

Unfortunately, at that exact moment when Adriana had put her arms about the baronet's shoulders, Lord Borland entered the drawing room. As he saw his friend embrace the young lady in such an intimate fashion, he wasn't the least surprised. What did shock him was that Miss Addington seemed to be enjoying the gentleman's attentions. Her arms positively lingered around his neck. The viscount shut the door with undue thrust, causing it to slam. The couple started and moved apart.

To William's amazement, the lady showed not the least embarrassment. She turned and held up her charm. "Sir Perrick has been as good as his word, my lord. I have my necklace back."

Seeing the expression on the viscount's face, Perry couldn't resist stirring the flames of jealousy, for it was clear to him that the viscount hadn't a clue to his true feeling for the beauty. "Allow me to put it on for you, Miss Addington."

His hands covered her fingers, lingering overlong as she held the treasure. But the lady hesitated as she gazed down at the necklace in her hand. "Sir, this chain is far finer than my old one. I do not think it proper I should accept such a gift from a gentleman."

Perry grinned and watched his old friend. "What say you, Will? Is it not my family's responsibility to replace what my half brother destroyed?"

By this time the viscount had moved to where the pair

stood near the windows. He surveyed the chain in question. He very much wanted to tell the young lady not to accept such an expensive token from a rake, but in truth he knew his friend to be in the right. As head of the family, he did owe the lady a replacement.

Gruffly, William said, "There can be no suggestion of impropriety . . . at least about the necklace." He glowered at his friend, but Sir Perrick only laughed.

The baronet took the necklace from the lady and moved behind her, fastening the clasp. When he finished, he placed his hands on the young lady's shoulders and turned her to face him. "Perfect, my dear Miss Addington. Now all I need do is wrangle an invitation for dinner this evening so that I might admire you wearing your necklace. Then my day shall be complete."

William wasn't certain what had come over him, but he suddenly didn't like his friend at all. "Well, you cannot come to dinner, since we won't be here. We leave for Scotland after nuncheon."

Surprise registered on the young lady's face. "So soon, my lord. Are you certain you are ready for the journey?"

"I am quite fit. Don't you need to do some packing?"

Adriana, a bit befuddled by the news, turned and offered her hand to Sir Perrick. "May I thank you from the bottom of my heart for having recovered my medallion, sir?"

The baronet's hazel eyes twinkled. "I shall gladly take any part of a lady's heart she offers, Miss Addington. 'Tis a pity I shall have no time to enjoy it, since Will is taking you from our midst." He lifted the lady's hand to his lips, but his gaze was riveted on Borland, whose eyes seemed to be ablaze.

"Don't dither over the matter, Perry. We have much to do before we leave," Lord Borland snapped.

Adriana was suddenly aware of strange undercurrents in the room. She didn't know what was happening between the two friends. All she knew was the viscount appeared out of humor and the baronet seemed quite pleased with himself.

Having teased his friend sufficiently, Sir Perrick straightened and bid the viscount farewell and a safe journey. He promised to visit the next time he returned to the neighborhood, then departed.

The door had scarcely closed behind Sir Perrick before William vented his anger. "Miss Addington, I am not certain what you were taught about proper behavior in Italy, but a young lady does not throw herself into the arms of a gentleman in such a vulgar fashion in England."

Startled by the unwarranted attack, Adriana sputtered, "My lord, you mistake what you saw."

"Did I, or are Roman manners quite different from proper ones? In Italy is a lady allowed to dispense her favors freely?"

What was he accusing her of? she wondered. She began to become quite angry. "I was merely thanking the gentleman for having returned my necklace, my lord, nothing more. It was Sir Perrick who tried to take advantage of the situation."

"Thanking him!" William's ire was so great, he took a step toward the lady. "Then why have you not thanked me in such a manner, for I am your escort to Scotland?"

With that the gentleman suddenly pulled the lady into his arms and kissed her angrily.

Ten

As strong arms crushed her against a hard chest, Adriana stiffened in surprise at his lordship's unexpected kiss. But within moments she found the wonderful feel of his mouth covering hers melted her resistance. Her body seemed to mold to Borland's, and she experienced a rush of sensations totally unfamiliar to her yet exhilarating. But as quickly as the kiss had come, it ended.

She stood speechless, in a stupor of agreeable wonder at her first kiss. All she could think was she wanted him to embrace her again, to make her feel delightfully weak and tingling. Then her gaze moved from his lips to his blue eyes, which now held a hint of disapproval, but she wasn't certain if it was for his conduct or hers. She knew only that his look made her lose all joy at the embrace. Her cheeks warmed to a blush. She'd behaved like a wanton.

In a husky voice his lordship said, "You must forgive my uncalled-for conduct, Miss Addington. I don't know what came over me. You have my word I shall never again take such liberties." With that, he turned and walked to the door, where he paused with his hand on the lever, but he didn't look back. "Please be ready to leave for Scotland by one o'clock."

The viscount then quietly exited the room, leaving Adriana full of confused thoughts. Why had he kissed her? To punish her for having not been properly careful

with Sir Perrick? Or had he been jealous? But she
quickly dismissed that idea. Could one be jealous before
one was in love? There had certainly been no gentle affection in his kiss, but there had been heat and excitement. Had she just experienced passion? the innocent
girl wondered.

She moved to the window to stare at the rain, trying
to sort out her thoughts. Why had she responded so
eagerly to the man's touch? Was she the wanton she
thought, or . . . had she developed deeper feelings for
the gentleman? He was handsome, yet that affected her
opinion of him little. She'd discovered that beneath all
the proud and scholarly exterior was a good, decent man.
The incident when he had suggested they take the cat to
the countess proved he even owned a wry sense of humor.

He was a complicated man, not at all the type she
would have thought she would be drawn to. She'd seen
a vulnerable side to him as well, the night she'd read to
him in his bedchamber. Her heart began to race as she
remembered the way he'd watched her and the way it
had made her feel. Suddenly, in a moment of clarity of
her emotions, she knew she'd fallen in love with Lord
Borland.

Her knees grew weak at the notion and she sank into
a nearby chair. How could she have been so foolish? This
was a man who seemed to have some deep-rooted dis-
trust of women. She'd guessed that his mother, and to a
lesser degree his grandmother, had tried to manipulate
him. She'd seen with her own eyes the length females
would go to capture his title and money. And Adriana
knew she had been nothing but trouble and an inconvenience in his life.

She dropped her head into her hands, covering her
face. She'd managed to fall in love with the one man
who'd likely never return her affection.

Just then a knock sounded on the drawing room door. Adriana rose, struggling to regain her composure. At last she called for the visitor to enter.

Mrs. Raines came bustling into the room, her face a picture of distress. "Miss Addington, you are just the one I was hoping to see. I've just learned from Curtwood that his lordship intends to leave for Scotland this very day."

"I believe that is his wish, ma'am."

"We must do something to convince him he's not ready to travel. Dr. Burrell ordered that he wait until the end of the week, and now suddenly he is determined to depart this afternoon. Could you not convince him to stay?" The housekeeper looked at Adriana as if she held some sway over the gentleman.

Seeing the worried shadows in the woman's eyes, Adriana took the woman's hand. "Mrs. Raines, I heartily agree with you, but I don't foresee that I would be able to change the gentleman's mind." Especially not after what had just passed between them. "However, I always believe that one knows best what one can endure after an illness. So we must accept his lordship's confidence that he is well enough to make the journey. I promise that Nancy and I shall look after the gentleman should he suffer a relapse."

Appearing she would argue, Mrs. Raines paused when the door to the drawing room opened and Nick came bounding in. "Miss Addington, you must come to your room at once."

"What has happened?" Adriana remembered the last time the lad had summoned her. The event had ended in disaster.

"Nancy found Signora in the stables. She's 'ad the kittens. I 'elped bring 'em in out of the cold."

With a determined effort to distract herself from her woes, Adriana declared her desire to see the new litter.

She and Mrs. Raines followed Nick to her chamber, where they discovered Nancy had the gray feline and her new little ones safely settled into a basket near the fireplace. Signora was the proud mother of three new kittens—one gray, one black, and one white.

Adriana welcomed the discussion about what to name the tiny creatures. It kept her mind from dwelling on private thoughts of Lord Borland. Nick at last settled on Smoky, Midnight, and Snowball. After some minutes of admiring the new family, Mrs. Raines announced her duties awaited her, and she took Nick off with her, saying she had some errands for him.

Later, as the new mother and her kittens slept, Adriana changed into her blue traveling gown, which no longer carried his lordship's blood due to Nancy's skills. Despite her best effort to keep her thoughts from dwelling on his lordship, she couldn't resist questioning the maid.

"Nancy, do you think Lord Borland shall ever marry?"

Folding clothes to go into Adriana's portmanteau, the servant looked up and eyed the young lady thoughtfully. "Well, miss, 'tis very much his grandmother's wish, but he's always been steadfast in sayin' he's got an heir and don't need a wife. Can't say I blame him, what with the way his mother did her best to make his life exactly what *she* wanted it to be. By the time he was old enough to defy her, she had the consumption, and used her ill health as a powerful weapon to control the young man."

Nancy watched Adriana turn and gaze out the window thoughtfully, her expression bleak. Why, could it be that the child had fallen in love with his lordship? But the maid felt no joy at the notion because the gentleman was no young buck and seemed very much set against marrying. Then there was her ladyship pesterin' him at every turn to take a bride, which in Nancy's opinion always seemed to set one's back up against a scheme.

Still, Nancy didn't want to crush the lady's hopes.

"There is always the possibility he will get past his strong notions about females. They say love does strange things to people."

Adriana nodded. What the maid had told her explained much about this viscount's wish to avoid females. It made her want to go to him and wipe away all the years of his mother's manipulation, but that couldn't be done at this late date. The problem was with nearly every marriage-minded female pursuing him so blatantly, he'd only hardened his determination to keep women from his life.

Perhaps it was best that they leave for Scotland at once. The sooner there, the sooner the viscount would leave. That meant she wouldn't have to torture herself being with the one man who didn't seem to want a female in his life.

The library fire crackled and danced brightly in contrast to the foul weather. William sat in the familiar surroundings of the chamber, but this time he gleaned no comfort from his stacks of books. He hadn't even bothered to pick one up on his entry, instead going to the fireplace, where he still pondered his actions earlier in the drawing room. He'd behaved like a cad and he knew there was no excuse. Seeing Adriana in Perry's arms had made him insanely furious. Never had he experienced such a painful emotion before and hoped never to again. He'd spread his anger equally, thinking the young lady was as much to blame as his old friend. Hadn't he cautioned her about Perry and his lascivious ways? Yet she'd ignored his warning. But wasn't that just like a woman to pay no heed to good advice?

Feeling decidedly restless, William rose from the chair and moved to the window, peering out at the slow, steady rain. Should they leave for Scotland in these dreadful weather conditions? He'd blurted out the announced departure in anger, but even as he wanted to remain at the abbey, he knew they must go. Clearly, he couldn't control his actions around Miss Addington, and the sooner he deposited the young lady with his grandmother, the sooner she would be out of his life. He might at last find some semblance of peace in his own home, but what of his own heart?

The question startled him. Then he gave a bitter chuckle. He wanted Adriana as a man wants a woman, but that had little to do with his heart. Or so he told himself.

Just then a knock sounded at the library door. In truth, the viscount was happy not to have to peer too deeply into his own feelings, since he wasn't certain what they were. But he had a niggling feeling that if he did discover the truth, his entire ordered world might come crumbling down.

Thomas and Katy entered, the pair looking as if they'd won some prize at the local fair. "I have a request, my lord. I want to remain behind to marry Katy. If we have the banns read this Sunday, we'll be married in the new year."

"This is rather sudden, Thomas." William glanced at Katy, thinking that Thomas didn't know the young woman at all and only months ago she'd foolishly thought herself in love with his dastardly cousin, Randolph.

"My lord, I fell in love the moment I set eyes upon her." Thomas looked at the girl, and she giggled, then drew closer and stared at the viscount with a bit of fear.

William wasn't so sure this was the best thing for his household. An unhappy husband made for a poor employee. Many a man had married in haste, only to live to regret such a choice. There was still one major drawback. "Thomas, you know why . . . that is, you realize . . . Katy is . . ." The viscount wasn't sure how to broach the subject with a young man so much in love.

The footman nodded. "I know about the babe, my lord. I'd be right proud to be the papa of any child my Katy delivers. I love her, my lord."

Katy, her cheeks now pink from mortification, bit at her lip, then spoke bravely. "My lord, I do love Tommy. I was merely dazzled by . . ." Her voice trailed off, then she gazed into the footman's eyes. "Tommy takes care of me better'n even my own papa did. He is what I have always wanted."

Were they truly in love, as Katy now avowed, or was Thomas being tricked by a girl who needed a father for her baby? There could be no denying that both she and the babe would suffer the taunts of the locals without a marriage license.

As the viscount stood observing the couple in thoughtful silence, Katy stepped forward. "M'lord, I know me and Tommy ain't known one another very long, but I'll make him a good wife. Still, if you need him for yer trip, I'll gladly wait until after the holidays to have the banns read. I know we both owe you a great deal."

There was something so sincere in her pleading eyes that all William's doubts faltered. He knew he should warn his footman about the trials and tribulations he would face with a female in his life, but he didn't have the heart to dash the lad's joy. "That won't be necessary. Thomas, instruct Nick on his duties and he shall be the one to accompany me and may I wish you happy."

Katy impulsively kissed the viscount's cheek, then turned and threw herself into the arms of a beaming Thomas. Over his beloved's shoulder, the footman said, "I would hope that you will be as happy as I am one day, my lord."

After the pair departed, William wondered if he would ever be that happy. He knew there was very much a part of him that wanted Adriana Addington. She was beautiful and engaging, and she stirred feelings he never knew existed. But another part of him was still reluctant to have his life in so much constant upheaval as a lady of her temperament would bring. He closed his eyes and knew that he must find the strength to resist this physical attraction. He must reach deep in his soul and build a wall against her, for there was no doubt in his mind that they were too different to ever suit.

The journey to Scotland proceeded without any of the incidents that marred the earlier part of their trip. Adriana's first sight of Wother Castle came some day and a half hence in the late afternoon as the sun was about to disappear behind a nearby hill. The sight lightened her mood, for it meant that at least she would no longer be enclosed in a carriage with the coolly polite viscount. The gentleman's demeanor had been so formal since leaving Borland Abbey that he'd managed even to stifle Nick's lighthearted spirits.

Gazing out the coach window, she could see the castle was a great square Tudor-style building with large hexagonal turrets that jutted out on each of the four corners. The granite structure, bathed in the golden glow of the setting sun, looked like an oasis of warmth in the midst of the frosty Scottish countryside. The surrounding park had been landscaped in the more natural style of Capability Brown using hardwoods and evergreens to enhance the local countryside instead of the more formal gardens favored in most stately homes.

Adriana suspected that during the months of summer it would be quite beautiful, but in the bitter December cold there was a bleak remoteness that was frightening for someone who'd spent much of her life in teeming cities. It was going to take some time to become accustomed to her new life.

"Are you having second thoughts about being my grandmother's companion after seeing your new home?"

Adriana started as the gentleman spoke for the first time since they'd stopped for nuncheon. She gave a half-smile, glad he seemed less remote. "It is a bit more isolated than I would have expected but quite lovely just the same. I am certain I shall become accustomed to the place, given a little time."

"Perhaps not, for the current earl and his family prefer to live in Devonshire and have given over the castle to the dowager, Scotland being so far from the social rounds they're accustomed to. But you will soon see that you needn't worry about the remoteness during the holidays. I do assure you that if I know my grandmother, she will have invited so many people for Christmas that you will look forward to a walk outdoors, just to have some time to yourself."

At that moment the carriage drew up in front of the building and a flurry of gray-liveried footmen exited the great oak doors. Adriana soon found herself in a huge great hall, but save for a butler whom his lordship called Baxter, there seemed to be no one about.

"My lord, we are delighted to have you here at last. Her ladyship was beginning to worry what with Christmas Eve coming in two days and no word from you or the young lady."

The viscount pulled off his gloves. "We were delayed in Yorkshire. Where is everyone? I expected to find the castle overflowing with people. Has Boris's malady kept Grandmother from throwing her usual grand party?"

A hint of a smile tipped the butler's mouth. "Boris is quite well, my lord, and all the guests are in their rooms, changing for dinner, I believe. This year her ladyship limited the number of guests to only thirty."

Adriana's mind boggled at such a sum. Whatever did a lady need with a companion if she'd been managing such grand affairs on her own, but she made no comment.

As her gaze swept over the elegant antechamber, Adriana spotted a lady standing at the top of the staircase, and she knew instinctively she was looking at the Countess of Wotherford. The lady was small in stature and possessed snow-white hair beneath a tiny lace cap. She seemed to be observing them intently, a thoughtful expression on her face.

As her ladyship's gaze locked with Adriana's, a smile lit the older woman's face and she called, "You have come at last, my dears."

The countess made her way down the stairs slowly. She was fashionably dressed in a lilac silk evening gown with a white gauze overskirt worked with lilac flowers, the bodice trimmed with white lace and ribbons. When she drew closer, Adriana thought the countess appeared much younger than her years, and there was such a look of kindness in her blue eyes that many of Adriana's fears for her situation fled. The lady came directly to kiss Adriana's cheek and welcome her to Wother Castle.

The greeting between grandmother and grandson was somewhat strained, at least on the viscount's part.

"Grandmother, you are in looks as usual." His tone was cool and the countess was left in little doubt about his mood.

"So, I see you are still in rather bad skin about my sending dear Adriana to you. I do hope you have not played the bear the entire trip, else the child will think you are not fit company for man or beast."

Without waiting for his comment, the countess turned back to Adriana. "I cannot tell you how delighted I am to have you here. I have invited a great many people that I wish you to meet. Later you must tell me all about your mother and father and their life in Italy. How I shall miss dear Hugh."

"I miss him dreadfully, my lady." Adriana, even knowing what she did about the countess, liked this outspoken and energetic lady.

"Grandmother," the viscount interrupted the lady who'd been chattering a mile a minute. "We have just traveled over rather dreadful roads for the past two days. I think Miss Addington might wish to lie down before we dine and you begin besieging her with questions."

Lady Margaret eyed her grandson a moment, then nodded her agreement. "Why, that was what I was about to suggest. Nancy, show the young lady to the Rose Room, then let Angie do for her tonight so you might rest as well." Her ladyship then patted Adriana's hand. "Sleep as long as you like. I shall have dinner set back so you may take all the time you wish."

As Miss Addington and Nancy disappeared at the top of the stairs, William crossed his arms over his chest and glared at Lady Margaret. "I know what you are about, Grandmother."

The lady arched one graying brow. "I should think everyone does, dear boy. I do it every year at this time. It's called a house party." The countess gave a wicked chuckle and turned, making her way toward the nearest drawing room. She gestured for the viscount to follow. "Come, you must see what I have done for the entertainment of my guests this year."

"Don't play the innocent with me, madam." In two strides he'd caught up with the old lady. "I've made it perfectly clear I'm not interested in getting married. You might foist as many females as you know upon me and it won't change my opinion on the subject."

"Oh, you needn't worry about that any longer. I cannot deny that I had hopes in that direction, but having seen Adriana, I realize that the two of you would not suit in the least. I can see it in her lively eyes. She needs an out-and-outer. A gentleman who will allow her to enjoy life's adventures, even as he has. 'Tis fortunate that I have invited several young gentlemen for Christmas who would be well suited to the lovely girl."

"An out-and-outer? Why would Miss Addington want such a man? Any proper gentleman could be a good husband to the young lady." William didn't want to watch a crowd of fashionable young bucks dangling after Adriana. "Oh, for the love of heaven, cease your matchmaking altogether, Grandmother. Leave both Miss Addington and me in peace."

They entered the Queen's Drawing Room as the gentleman made his pronouncement. The countess, ignoring her grandson's command, said, "Now, what think you of this?" The lady gestured at a great evergreen that stood beside the fireplace.

The viscount froze for a moment, startled by the sight. "Gad, madam, why have you put a tree in the house?" He stared at the great spruce, which went from floor to near the ceiling, momentarily distracted from the subject of Miss Addington. On the branches stood unlit white candles tied with red ribbons. Hanging from various branches all over the tree were bright red apples. He was beginning to think his grandmother was all about in her head in her old age.

"It's the German custom to celebrate Christmas with a tree. The candles represent the stars that guided the Wise Men and the fruit the gifts they carried. I had been hearing for years that Queen Charlotte always has such a tree at Windsor, and Lady Marchington told me it is quite true, for she saw it with her own eyes. So I wanted to try the custom this year."

"You are English, Grandmother. We burn trees at Christmas, remember the Yule Log. You'll be lucky if you don't burn down the castle should you light all those candles."

The countess clucked softly as she put her hands on her hips and stared at the viscount. "Well, my boy, I would never have thought it, but here you are, starting to sound just like your mother."

William was stunned into utter speechlessness by the accusation.

Suddenly across the room a head appeared above one of the sofas. A handsome young man, his black curls skillfully arranged in artful disarray appeared to have been lying down on the couch. He stretched and yawned, then seemed to realize he wasn't alone. He rose and bowed to his hostess. One could see his clothes were expensively made, and his athletic physique suggested he was much involved with all the sports that engaged fashionable young men. No doubt the man was considered a nonpareil by his friends.

"Lady Margaret, pray excuse my rumpled state. I came in here for a moment's quiet after a spirited game of billiards with Shipton and fell right into the arms of Morpheus, as they say. Ain't late for supper, am I?"

"Not at all, dear boy. Lord Peter, may I present my grandson, Viscount Borland. William, the Marquess of Binfield."

The young man bowed again, then groped about for his quizzing glass and eyed the viscount rudely. "You're that bookish fellow, are you not?"

"The very one." As William said the words, for the first time he didn't care that there was a bit of distaste in the young man's question. It really didn't matter what others thought of him anymore.

The marquess's face puckered in thought. "I read a book once—after I left Oxford, that is. It mustn't have been very good, for I cannot remember the name of it. Waste of time in my opinion to be reading about dungeons and hysterical females. Now, horses, that is something to keep a man's thoughts occupied. I never miss what Mr. Pierce Egan writes about the Fancy."

Her ladyship chuckled. "It is getting late, my lord. You must hurry and change, for the gong will ring in an hour and Cook has outdone herself this evening."

The young marquess's face brightened. "I say, don't want to miss a good meal. Your servant, Borland." With that, the young man exited.

The door had scarcely closed, when her ladyship, eyeing her grandson, said, "What a prospect for Adriana. Fifty thousand a year and a title as well."

Before William could voice the least objection, his grandmother was at the door, saying, "I have duties to attend, and you need to change as well. I shall see you in the dining room." So saying, she hurried out of the drawing room, leaving her grandson furious.

"If that horse-mad dullard is an out-and-outer, then I am the King of Cashmere."

Eleven

"Tell me everything, Nancy." Lady Margaret gestured for the maid to take a seat in the worn red damask chair. The countess had chosen the housekeeper's private rooms, where they wouldn't be disturbed in the over-crowded castle. While she might tell her grandson that she'd given up on matchmaking, she had a plan. "I want to know about their first meeting and everything that happened on the journey."

Nancy's steps slowed as she neared the seat, not wanting to disappoint her ladyship. "My lady, I know you've got your hopes set on a match between Miss Addington and the viscount, but I'm thinkin' the gentleman is likely to cut off his nose just to spite his own face before he'll fall in with your wishes."

"What do you mean? Does he dislike Adriana? How is that possible? She is delightful, as I knew any child of Hugh's would be."

Nancy settled into the chair, then gave a sigh and fussed with the fabric of her ecru print skirts. Avoiding her mistress's gaze, she said, " 'Tain't that. I just think he's determined to do the opposite of what you want just to prove he's his own man."

Her ladyship sat back and gazed into the fire. "I have begun to suspect the same thing." Then the lady sat up again, a smile lighting her face. "That is why I have changed my strategy. But tell me, what do you think he truly thinks about Adriana?"

Realizing the countess couldn't be dissuaded from the idea of a union between the pair, Nancy said, "Fact is, I'd sometimes catch him gazin' at her and those looks could make a decent woman blush. He's taken with her, but, my lady, Miss Addington ain't exactly a pattern card of proper conduct. You need to find someone a bit less spirited for a quiet, studious gentleman like his lordship."

Her ladyship sat up straighter. "Are you telling me my godson's daughter behaves like common baggage?"

Nancy's eyes widened. "No, my lady, she's genteel from her lovely black locks to the tips of her toes. But she's not some milk-and-water miss who hangs on a gentleman's every word. Got a mind of her own, she does. The young lady don't hesitate to offer her opinion or even take matters into her own hands. Independent-like is what I call her. Truth to tell, she's just plain more high-spirited than the gentleman is used to."

A thoughtful expression settled on Lady Margaret's face. Was Adriana too lively for the likes of William? Sounded exactly like the perfect match, for clearly the girl needed someone with a cooler head to keep her in check. Convinced she was in the right in her thinking, the countess wanted to find out all about how the pair had gotten along. "Tell me about their first meeting. Did he admire her?"

Nancy began at the beginning, telling of the tumultuous encounter in London and all the events that soon followed. At first the countess heard nothing good, the pair being quarrelsome with each other in the library, but soon the maid had her ladyship smiling at Miss Addington's barbed comments to his lordship's traveling library.

Occasionally the countess would chuckle or ask some question about her grandson's reaction to the young lady.

Upon hearing about Katy, her ladyship tsked, then said, "I told William how it would be having a cad for an heir. But in truth that turn of events only helps with my campaign to get my grandson married. Maybe at last he realizes he needs to produce a proper heir." The countess paused a moment, then quietly asked, "Did he do right by this unfortunate young woman?"

Nancy assured the lady that not only had he taken the fallen female to the abbey, but she was to be married in the new year to one of his lordship's footmen. The maid returned to the story.

Hearing about his lordship's part in young Nick's rescue and cleaning, Lady Margaret's face settled into skeptical lines. When Nancy assured her it was quite true, her ladyship smiled and said, "Extraordinary, but a good sign. I wondered what Will was doing with such a young lad in attendance."

Upon learning about the party being waylaid by highwaymen and her grandson's injury, Lady Margaret rose and began to pace. The lady was full of remorse about Lord Borland's injury, but then she reasoned that such a robbery could happen at any time on the roads in the country. On a calmer note she settled once again beside the fireplace.

Finally Nancy finished her tale. "I was beginnin' to have hopes that the gentleman had fallen prey to the young lady's charms, but something happened that last mornin'. Some local baronet arrived and his lordship's been as stiff as new starched linen with Miss Addington ever since."

"Someone from Yorkshire? Was it his neighbor, Sir Perrick Kingston?"

The maid nodded, then her ladyship sat back in the chair and smiled knowingly. She'd occasionally seen Perry in town but more often heard tales of his exploits with women. What had happened to put William in the sulks? Had jealousy put him out of frame? Had the rake taken a fancy to Adriana? Then the lady frowned, or had Adriana fallen prey to the charms of a rake?

Realizing that the maid was watching her closely, Lady Wotherford said, "That will be all, Nancy. You have done extremely well. If you should like to visit your family in Edinburgh for the holidays, I shall have one of the grooms drive you in the morning."

"Beggin' your pardon, my lady, but I'd like to stay at the castle and see for myself how it all turns out with the lady and the gentleman."

The countess rose. "Of course you may stay. In truth, I have a plan." The lady explained what she intended, and Nancy agreed to do all in her power to help.

The servant left her ladyship in the small room just off the kitchens. As the door closed, shutting out the noisy sounds of preparation for the evening meal, Lady Margaret gazed into the fire, her thoughts centered on her new scheme. She knew it was possible that all her designing efforts might blow up in her face, but she was willing to risk such an explosion for the sake of dear William.

On that thought, the countess rose, heading to the drawing room and her duties as hostess. It was going to be a busy few days.

The Long Gallery at Wother Castle, the walls lined with two centuries of family portraits, was filled with as many fashionable people that December night as any London drawing room during the height of the Season. Lady Margaret was a notable hostess whose invitations were much coveted and rarely declined.

William stood in the entry of the room, anxiously searching through the crowd of elegantly dressed guests for Miss Addington. He felt it his duty to warn her that his grandmother had taken it upon herself to find the young lady a husband. He remembered from his earlier conversation that marriage held no part in her desires. Adriana Addington was unlike most females he'd ever met. Like him, she would dislike someone else trying to direct the manner in which she was to live her life.

He recognized many of the people gathered in the room from previous holidays in Scotland and the Season in Town. As usual, there was a glittering array of Society's elite as well as many of the local residents of Kelso. He nodded polite acknowledgments, hoping that none would come to talk with him until he'd had a moment to speak privately with Miss Addington.

He spied the young lady in her rose-pink gown. Her hair was done elaborately with small pink roses, no doubt a gift from his grandmother. He started toward her, but to his dismay a large hand clamped on his shoulder.

"Borland, 'tis glad I am to see you've come to Kelso. You have delighted your grandmother." William turned around and found Baron MacEwan, the countess's nearest neighbor, stood smiling at him. The gentleman's face was fully covered with a salt-and-pepper-hued beard, but his head held a shine like the nearby polished tabletops. William had always liked the baron, who'd been in the army before stepping into the shoes of his late brother. The old soldier had some amazing tales about life in India.

But at this moment, William had a greater interest in what was going on across the room. There was a strange tightening in his gut as he took note that the men all appeared to be vying for a young lady's attention.

"Lord MacEwan, I had not expected to see you at my grandmother's party."

The baron looked around, making certain there was no one near to hear him, then in a lowered voice he said, "I detest dressing up like some ridiculous Town Pink. But my niece and nephew are staying at the Hall since their mama died last spring, and Lady Margaret says I need to take them out and about. So here I am, my feet aching in these new buckled pumps Gerald talked me into the last time we were in Edinburgh. A cursed nuisance doing the pretty at my age, but one must do one's duty."

How often had William heard the last portion of that very statement from his own grandmother. "You would do better to seek counsel from someone other than the countess, sir. Her philosophy is to interfere in others' affairs whenever possible." William's gaze never left Adriana. He heard her husky laugh and suddenly wished it had been only for him and not that collection of dandies, coxcombs, and puppies who surrounded her.

The baron chuckled. "Lady Margaret does have definite ideas about matters, to be sure. But I've always found her advice to be sound."

The lady under discussion, spying her grandson, began advancing on the gentleman at that moment from across the room. William instinctively knew he wouldn't get within two feet of Miss Addington if his grandmother didn't wish it. She was perhaps the most managing female he'd ever met save his own dearly departed mother.

"There you are, dear boy. Come with me, I want you to meet MacEwan's young relations."

The lady locked her arm with his and drew him farther away from where Miss Addington appeared to be holding court. He was led down to the bottom of the room, where they joined a group of three, a young man and woman in conversation with an old acquaintance of William's.

The Right Reverend Montague Hart, Lord Bishop of Yorkshire, greeted him warmly, inquiring how things were at Borwood Abbey. The viscount was then introduced to Miss Naomi Lowe, and her brother Gerald. As the conversation turned to the party and whether there would be snow for Christmas, William observed Lord

MacEwan's female relation closely and with a bit of suspicion.

Had his grandmother invited this young lady as another prospective bride for him? Then he almost laughed out loud. He was becoming positively irrational about the countess's matchmaking to think that every female had been invited just to entice him to pick a bride.

As his gaze swept the drab female, the viscount realized his grandmother would never have chosen such a woman to try to lure him to the altar. But as he inspected the young lady closer, he discovered that she wasn't truly plain, she'd merely done little to enhance her looks. Her blonde hair had been pulled back into a severe knot at the back of her head. She was dressed in a simple blue gown with an unfashionably high collar with a white lace ruff about the neck and long sleeves. Her shapely mouth drew into a thin line of disapproval as she listened to the countess explain what was planned for the guests. A look of discontent in the young lady's blue eyes made it evident that she wanted to be anywhere but at Wother Castle at that exact moment.

Within a matter of minutes the viscount's suspicions returned in full force when his grandmother managed to spirit away all the others in the group, leaving William with little choice but to converse with the young woman. As he searched for something to say, Miss Lowe surprised him by boldly eyeing him.

"I understand from your grandmother you are a well-read gentleman, my lord."

"I have an extensive library and I do read as often as I can. And do you enjoy books?"

Miss Lowe gave a brittle laugh. "I am considered a bluestocking, sir, and am quite proud of that fact. I am the mental equal of any man." She glared at him as if daring him to argue.

William was left bereft of speech, not by what she

said but at her belligerent tone. He'd heard of the Blue-stocking societies of females who studied all manner of subjects, but this was the first one of their number he'd ever encountered. He suddenly wondered if they were all quite so testy as Miss Lowe.

The lady continued without waiting for any comment. "I should like very much to study in Edinburgh to become a physician, but my uncle tells me they would never allow a female entry there. He deludes himself that I shall marry and become a dutiful drudge for some man, since I shall not put my studies aside for any man."

The lady then went into what she'd planned to read over the course of the next few weeks. As she rambled on, William realized this was the kind of scholarly and disciplined female he'd imagined would be right for him should he ever decide to marry. But there was nothing in this bitter lady that appealed to him in the least.

His gaze strayed to Miss Addington, still surrounded by flirting beaus. The lady was the opposite of everything Miss Lowe was, and opposite of everything he thought he wanted, yet still he desired her. The logic of that totally escaped him at the moment.

Across the room, Adriana was bored despite the crowd of gentlemen hovering, determined to amuse her. When Lord Binfield asked her a second time if she would drive out with him on the following day, she realized that she'd scarcely heard a word spoken since Lord Borland entered the room. Why did he stare at her with such an intense gaze? Did the viscount wish to speak with her, or was it merely wishful thinking on her part?

To Adriana's disappointment, Lady Wotherford had led the viscount and the man who'd joined him to the opposite end of the room. Within what seemed to be minutes, Adriana could see that the viscount was alone with a rather prim-looking female who appeared to have a great deal to say to the gentleman. Was her ladyship once again matchmaking? Had the countess seen in an instant that Adriana and the viscount would never suit?

"I say, Miss Addington, you seem to be woolgathering," Lord Binfield chided. "Which is it to be? A drive in my new curricle, or riding with Shipton here."

Adriana stared at the two earnest young men, both moderately handsome and wealthy, who were awaiting her decision. She gave a rather hollow laugh, knowing she didn't wish to go with anyone but Lord Borland, and he wasn't likely to ask her to set foot in one of his carriages ever again.

"Gentlemen, I cannot make any plans until I know what Lady Margaret wishes me to do in the morning. You must remember that I am not a guest but her ladyship's companion."

The young men's protests were interrupted by the announcement that dinner was to be served. To Adriana's dismay, she discovered that they were also her dinner partners. She wasn't certain if it was fatigue from the day's journey or her distraction of watching Lord Borland and the lady in the prim blue gown at the opposite end of the table that made her such a miserable conversationalist. All she knew was that she was hardly glad to retire to her chamber at the end of the evening.

Eager to begin her duties, Adriana arose early on the following morning. She learned from Nancy that her ladyship had requested her presence as soon as she was dressed.

She knocked on the door of the countess's chambers and was bid to enter. Opening the door, she checked at the threshold and stared in amazement at the unusually decorated room. The Dowager Countess of Wotherford's chamber looked like the interior of a bedouin tent. Well, mayhap a lady bedouin, for the fabric that was draped from the center of the room to the outer walls, then to the floor, was a soft pink.

Her ladyship sat drinking hot chocolate in a large canopied bed done in white hangings with pink rosebuds worked into the weblike gossamer fabric. A lacy pink counterpane lay over the end of the bed, and Oriental rugs of deep burgundy and pink covered the floor. The whole effect was a bit overpowering.

In the midst of all this feminine decoration lay a great, hairy, tan dog who appeared more suited to roaming the outdoors than perched at the feet of a lady of Quality. The great beast rose and padded across the floor to inspect his mistress's newest visitor. Adriana instinctively stepped back.

"Don't be afraid, my dear. Boris is very large but as gentle as a lamb and too old to be of any bother to anyone. I am hoping you shall be friends, for I should like you to walk him every morning."

Adriana gazed skeptically at the large dog, then reached out and patted the wiry-looking fur, which was surprisingly soft. To her amusement, the dog leaned his head against her side as she stroked him. He was quite as docile as Signora had been despite his great size.

After making friends with her ladyship's dog, Adriana spent the next hour or more answering questions about her father and life in Italy. In turn she heard about a paternal grandmother she'd never known. Then the conversation took an abrupt twist.

"Well, my dear, you have spent nearly a week in my grandson's company and Nancy tells me you had an interesting journey. What think you of William?"

To her chagrin, Adriana's cheeks warmed at such a direct question. "I think him . . . a very good sort of person. If you have heard of our adventures, you know about Miss Hunt and about Nick. He has done all that was proper for them."

The countess laughed and made a dismissive gesture. "I was delighted to hear of his kindness, but that tells me nothing of your feelings. Do you like him?"

Adriana hesitated a moment, uncomfortable with the subject. Realizing there could be no escaping the determination of a hardened matchmaker, she looked straight into Lady Margaret's eyes. "I do, very much, and because I do, I won't be involved in any schemes to trick the gentleman into marriage, my lady."

"Nor would I ask you to, for I should never wish my grandson to marry a schemer, even though his grandfather did." Her ladyship laughed at the expression on Adriana's face. "I have no illusions about myself, dear child. But I know my grandson well, and I think the right woman would make him far happier than he has ever been. His books offer knowledge and safe comfort but not happiness."

Adriana rose and went to the window. "No doubt you are correct, but I don't think I am the type of woman who would suit such a man, my lady. Our temperaments are too dissimilar."

"That is balderdash, Adriana. It has always been my experience that opposites attract. Why, my husband loved the outdoors, horses, and collecting old coins, none of which interested me in the least. I adored art, music, and the Season, yet we were very happy together. Sameness is boring."

Looking back at the countess, Adriana became curious. "But surely you must have had something in common."

"We both loved travel and entertaining friends here at the castle, but most important, we loved each other. Now, I shall give you one bit of advice on the subject of love, then I will say no more about it, for you must come to your own decision about what you want."

The countess paused a moment, listening to the sounds of laughing voices in the hall. "My guests seem to be up and stirring. I must dress and see to their entertainment."

Adriana, eager to hear what her ladyship was about to say, reminded her, "And that bit of advice?"

"Oh, yes, 'tis my belief that a gentleman always wants most what he cannot have, especially when it concerns a lady."

At that moment, the wolfhound rose and went to scratch at the chamber door. The countess seemed to have put the very personal conversation from her mind as she'd promised. Without any other comment about the viscount, she threw back the covers and said, "Boris is ready for his walk. Dress warmly, my dear, for it is frightfully cold here, and don't let him keep you out too long. Give him to Baxter when you return. The rest of the day is yours to do with as you wish. There is a lead there beside the door, and do ring for my maid before you go."

Thus dismissed, Adriana left, her thoughts dwelling on exactly what good Lady Wotherford's advice would be to her. It wasn't as if she'd been dangling after Lord Borland. Then she remembered the kiss in his drawing room. She'd been as eager as a lightskirt. What had he thought of her after that?

After donning her bonnet and cape, Boris's energetic tug on the leash made Adriana realize she must concentrate on matters at hand. The dog pulled her down the hall, seemingly eager to be outside. At the head of the stairs she encountered Lord Binfield. It was all she could do to hold the animal in check.

"I say, Miss Addington, that is a capital animal. I wonder how it would do fox hunting."

"I think it was bred for hunting wolves, my lord, but it's a bit old to do either."

The marquess shrugged his shoulders. "Pity, for I should like to give him a go. My guess is he would leave

Lynn Collum

the hounds behind with those long legs. Speaking of going, what say you to a drive in my sporting carriage a bit later?"

On a whim that she couldn't even explain to herself, Adriana said, "I should enjoy seeing the local countryside."

"By George, I shall send for my phaeton at once." With that, the gentleman dashed down the stairs.

Boris began to tug on the leash as if he meant to pursue the marquess. Adriana found herself pulled rapidly down the grand staircase at a startling speed. Thankfully, a footman leapt into action and opened the front door. In a flash she and Boris flew through the portal and out onto the front drive. The great lumbering dog veered right, and the young lady was at nearly a run as the animal made for some unknown destination.

All Adriana could do was hold onto the leash for dear life and pray that she didn't stumble as the dog hurtled toward the nearest field.

William gave the reins of the horse he'd borrowed from his grandmother's stables to a groom, then turned and strolled toward the castle. The early morning solitary ride had done little to clear his head about his grandmother's matchmaking efforts. He had few doubts that Miss Lowe had been the countess's alternative if things hadn't gone as she'd planned with Miss Addington. His grandmother was never likely to change, and he would be better advised to ignore her games and stratagems than rage against them. When she wasn't pestering him to take a wife, she was in truth full of amazing wisdom and insights on a variety of other subjects.

Rounding the north turret at the front of the castle, the viscount halted in amazement at what he saw. Boris was galloping straight at William—that was the only way to describe the gait on an animal that size. Hanging on to the dog's leash for dear life was Miss Addington, a look of sheer desperation on her lovely face.

In an instant William stepped into the animal's path and shouted, "Heel."

Boris obediently slid to a stop and settled on his haunches, but with her uncontrolled momentum Miss Addington kept going and slammed straight into the viscount, causing him to stagger backward a few steps. He managed to remain upright and still held on to her. The young lady clutched his jacket and laid her head upon his chest, gasping for breath and gratefully muttering, "Thank you, sir."

William's body betrayed him, responding to her softness. Frustrated by his reaction, he put her from him, then took the dog's leash from her hand. "Ah, Miss Addington, there is nothing like a leisurely stroll in the country, is there?"

Adriana, unable to gauge the gentleman's mood despite the jest, merely laughed breathlessly at the absurdity of calling that a leisurely stroll. After a moment to recover herself, she said, "I don't think I'm going to be able to walk Boris as her ladyship wishes. He is quite a handful."

"You have been with the countess? She was the one who told you to walk this brute?"

Adriana noted that he never once looked at her, keeping his gaze on the dog as he stroked the animal's head.

"She did. She wishes me to walk him every morning."

The viscount straightened. "Out of the question, Miss Addington. I will speak to my grandmother about the matter. You could have been badly hurt."

For once Adriana didn't argue. "Thank you, my lord."

At last he looked at her, but there was a shuttered quality to his blue eyes, as if he wanted to keep her at a distance. "I have been wanting to speak with you since last night. I feel I should warn you that my grandmother has decided to practice her matchmaking skills on you as she tries with me. I believe she thinks the Marquess of Binfield an excellent catch."

Adriana laughed, realizing at once what the countess had been up to, but all she said was "He *is* a very amusing young man."

Lord Borland's brows rose for just a fraction of a second before his face again became a polite mask. "I had no idea you were so eager to find a husband, Miss Addington."

"I'm not, my lord. But neither am I *avoiding* finding love by hiding from it. I would guess that such feelings very often come when we least expect them or want them."

Before William could respond to her implication that he was avoiding love, a sporting carriage came bowling up the drive from the stables. Lord Binfield drew the matched set of chestnuts to a halt, then rose, bracing his boot on the splash board while expertly keeping his team in check. He gallantly extended a hand to the lady. "Are you ready, Miss Addington?"

Adriana smiled innocently at the viscount. "I am, if Lord Borland would be so kind as to walk Boris a bit, then return him to the butler for me."

Giving a stiff bow, William watched as the marquess helped the lady into his carriage, then after a jaunty tip of his hat the young gentleman put his vehicle in motion.

William's gut tightened at the sight of Adriana smiling at that coxcomb Binfield as he masterfully tooled his phaeton until it disappeared over a small hill. Why was she out driving with such a man? The viscount knew Lord Binfield would be his grandmother's ideal for a husband—dashing, charming, and adept with women. Had Adriana fallen prey to the young nonpareil's charms?

And why did it bother him so to see her in the man's company?

Then he remembered her earlier charge. Was she right? Had he spent his life hiding from love? Before he could give the matter due thought, Boris gave a sharp tug on the leash, nearly pulling the viscount off his feet.

"Oh, very well, come on, you motley beast. I shall walk you, and I do mean walk, not run."

Twelve

Christmas Eve dawned cold and overcast, a steady but light snowfall slowly blanketing the countryside. Yet the weather did little to dampen the enthusiasm of the guests for the planned activities of the day.

At breakfast Lady Margaret announced she would need two separate parties of volunteers to help prepare the final decorations for Christmas Day. One group would ride south and undertake the task of finding a suitable Yule Log. The other group, accompanied by several footmen with a sledge, would go toward the River Tweed, where they might gather holly, ivy, and privet to decorate the drawing rooms and great hall.

Most of the older guests, especially the ladies, begged off from the outings, preferring to stay in the warmth of the castle to gossip and play cards. With the plans set, the younger guests, chattering about which group to join, retired to dress suitably for the cold, Scottish climate.

Lady Margaret surveyed her grandson, who'd remained seated at the table as the room emptied. "So, do you plan to join in the gaiety, William, or remain at the castle with the elders?"

The viscount's mouth curved into some semblance of a smile. There could be little doubt he recognized his grandmother's heavy touch in her barbed comment. "I shall remain to huddle near the fire with the rest of the old dotards."

The dowager's mouth twitched, but she said, "Unfortunate, since I am certain Miss Lowe might like a strong gentleman to carry her cut greenery back to the sledge."

Leaning back in his chair, the viscount shook his head. "Then you do not know the lady in the least. My guess would be that Miss Lowe is convinced she could carry her cuttings better than any mere gentleman. Don't pin your hopes on that female, for I'm quite certain should I take leave of my senses and offer for her, she wouldn't have me. She as much as informed me of the matter on our first meeting. As to joining your party, I have little interest in standing about in the cold all morning with a group of chattering chits."

The countess merely shrugged. " 'Tis a pity about Miss Lowe. I was certain I had found the perfect lady for you."

William pushed himself back from the table and quickly rose. "Grandmother, I beg of you, cease your scheming. Miss Lowe has no more wish for a match than I do. Only I shall know what will suit me in this matter." The gentleman kissed his grandmother. "Pray excuse me, but I shall be in the library if you have need of me."

Her ladyship's guests stood clustered in the great hall as William strode through the boisterous crowd to the library. He couldn't explain it, but ever since his conversation with Miss Addington the previous morning, he'd been out of sorts. He'd been weighing her accusation back and forth in his mind. Was he afraid of love? Had he isolated himself with his books and studies in an effort to protect himself from emotions?

The gentleman, deep in his own thoughts, passed through the hall without paying much heed to anyone. He opened the library door and disappeared from sight.

* * *

Adriana sighed. She'd hoped that Lord Borland would join them in what she'd learned was the castle's Christmas tradition, but the gentleman seemed even more distracted than usual. Lord Binfield soon arrived, trying to cajole her into going with him to hunt for the Yule Log, but she refused, saying she preferred to help with the decorations.

Watching the marquess's departing back, she almost wished that she could be fascinated with such a handsome, wealthy lord, for it would greatly ease her family's financial woes. But she could never marry for money, nor would Amy expect it of her. The truth was she found him very pleasant but very boring with his talk of carriage, horses, and racing.

She put the young man from her mind and drew on her gloves. Nick appeared at her side as she was doing the button on her cape.

"Ain't 'is lordship a-comin'?"

"I don't think so."

Disappointment descended on the boy's freckled face. "I was 'opin' to go with you, miss. This 'ere bringin' 'ome of greenery sounds like fun."

She ruffled his blond hair. "I am certain that Lord Borland won't mind if you go as my personal footman. There will be someone here to see to his wants should a need arise. Inform Baxter you are accompanying me and he will take care of matters."

The boy grinned, then dashed over to do as the lady had suggested. Within minutes, the guests poured out of the castle into the snow flurries and cold. The larger party boarded a collection of carriages to go south to find a suitable Yule Log. After the merry group left, only four women remained behind to do the cutting of the greenery—Adriana, Miss Lowe, Miss Patton, the spinster daughter of a retired colonel, and Lady Peters, a newly married young woman who lived in one of the neighboring estates.

The sledge arrived, pulled by a great dappled-gray horse whose traces were wrapped with ivy and bells. The ladies climbed on board, hanging on to the sides, for there was no place to sit in the cart designed for carrying wood. Three sturdy footmen and Nick climbed on the rear, then the groom set the horse in motion, but with runners instead of wheels the vehicle moved at a modest pace, for the snow was scarcely an inch deep.

Lady Margaret, standing in the castle doorway, waved at the departing guests, calling, "Be sure to look for a bit of mistletoe. It is very difficult to find in these parts, but we must have some if we are to have a Kissing Bough."

Despite her disappointment that Lord Borland had chosen not to join the party, Adriana determined to enjoy her first Christmas in Britain. As the sledge moved through the countryside, the bells jingling merrily, she took note of several picturesque spots that she wished to visit later with her sketchbook. Beside her, Miss Patton and Lady Peters chatted companionably, but Miss Lowe seemed to find no enjoyment in their outing, her face appearing a sullen mask as she stared ahead.

Hoping to draw the young woman from her dark mood, Adriana asked, "Is this your first Christmas in Scotland, Miss Lowe?"

The lady stared at her, seeming to take her measure and finding Adriana wanting. "And my last if I have my way about the matter, but then, females are rarely ever heeded even when they do have two thoughts to rub together in their heads." The lady's eyes narrowed as she added, "Which most don't."

It was plain to Adriana that the young lady was at Wother Castle very much against her wishes. Uncertain what to say, Adriana merely remarked, "A woman's lot has never been easy."

"Too true" was all Miss Lowe grudgingly vouched before turning her gaze back to the scenery.

At last the sledge came to a halt on a rise above the river, which cut a dark swath through the white landscape. All at once Miss Lowe seemed to take over, appearing more the army officer than a young lady of Quality. "We must be organized to finish this business quickly." She ordered the footmen to accompany the ladies, then told Miss Patton and Lady Peters to take their shears and go to a stand of trees that bordered the river.

"I have walked beside this river often. You should be able to find more than enough of the botanical cuttings that Lady Margaret requires." Then the young woman turned her commanding gaze on Adriana.

"You and I shall have the difficult task of searching for mistletoe. Have you ever seen the elusive plant? Do you know what it looks like?"

About to respond that mistletoe grew even in Italy, Adrian halted when Nick stepped to her side and piped, "I'll 'elp 'er find a good bunch, miss. A branch with lots of berries."

Miss Lowe glared at the child as if she meant to forbid him to come, but at that moment Adriana put her arm around the boy's shoulder, a challenge in her amber eyes. "Lead the way, Miss Lowe. Nick and I shall follow."

With a rather annoyed sigh, the young lady seemed to accept the lad, then turned and set off south, following what appeared to be a path along the bank. The surrounding boulders had kept the snow light in the area, leaving the path accessible. Adriana and Nick followed behind. Some fifty yards after they'd begun, Miss Lowe appeared to overcome her pique and called over her shoulder to look especially closely at the oaks, birches, or any other hardwoods where the small green plant attached itself and grew.

They had traveled nearly a half-mile when they came to a stone fence and wooden bridge that appeared to be the edge of the Wotherford estate. A road lay beyond the low stone barrier, then another dense woods, which were unenclosed.

Adriana was beginning to think they wouldn't find any mistletoe, when Nick shouted, "There be some, up in that tree on the other side of the road. I'll climb up and bring it down. You ladies sit 'ere on the fence by the road and rest."

Before she could urge him to be careful, the lad had climbed the embankment, then scaled the low fence and dashed across the road. After trudging up the steep bank, she gladly settled on the neatly piled stones. While catching her breath, she watched as Nick worked his way up the branches of the oak tree.

"Do you think that one bunch of mistletoe will be enough for Lady Margaret?" she asked Miss Lowe, who'd just made it up the embankment.

The young lady cupped her hands above her eyes to keep the snowflakes from being in the way. "I would guess it would depend on how many berries are on the branch. The lad must hurry, or we will be stranded out here if the snow becomes too deep."

"He is going as fast as he safely can." Adriana kept her gaze riveted on Nick, not wanting to call and urge him to hurry for fear he might have an accident in his rush. He was a good way into the other woods, and as he climbed the tree, he became obscured by the leaves.

Just to make conversation with her sullen companion, Adriana asked, "Why is everyone so concerned with how many berries are on the branch?

Miss Lowe settled on the fence, a distasteful expression on her face. "Because the mistletoe is attached to the Kissing Bough. Each person who wants a Christmas kiss must pluck a berry first. When all the berries are gone, there are no more kisses permitted under the Bough."

Adriana knew whom she wanted to pluck a berry and kiss her, but she suspected that Lord Borland scorned such traditions. He'd shown little evidence of being in the Christmas spirit since they'd arrived at Wother Castle.

The thunderous pounding of hooves echoed in the distance, and the women gazed down the road, but the snow, which had been getting progressively heavier as the morning passed, cloaked the rider. There was something about the eerie sound of the hoofbeats in their snowy isolation that gave Adriana a feeling of impending doom. She tried to tell herself she was being foolish, but she couldn't shake the feeling.

At last the horse was visible through the blanket of white flakes. They could see a man hunched over, riding hard, his black cape billowing out behind, a round hat pulled low, his face in shadow. At the last moment the rider saw the women beside the road and hauled on his reins, causing the horse to rear, then dance backward at the harsh handling. The animal veered to the opposite side of the road. The man's hat, brushed off by a low-hanging branch, exposed greasy reddish-blond hair.

The breath caught in Adriana's throat. She knew that she was once again staring into the evil eyes of the highwayman. Only now she knew him for who he was—Jack Kent.

"Well, ain't this me lucky day. I've run the little lady to grass what I've been most wanting to see since I was tossed into the goal. Where's his lordship? I'm wantin' him as well."

Adriana straightened, but her knees felt quite weak. "The gentleman is at the castle. You will have to settle for me."

With that, the man smirked with an evil grin. "I don't rightly think that'll be enough to satisfy me lust for vengeance . . . among other things."

A chill took hold of Adriana that went deep into her soul. With great effort she pushed the black thoughts away, knowing she wouldn't be able to act if she were frozen with terror. Staring at his face, she suddenly wondered how she could ever have mistaken Sir Perrick for this dastardly villain. The general look and configuration of the man's countenance was the same, but there was a cruel set to Kent's mouth that was missing in the baronet's, and the eyes had a cold look that could chill the bones.

Across the road, a branch in the oak tree shook ever so slightly. Adriana saw a flash of Nick's claret livery high in the tree. She forced herself to look in another direction, praying that Kent wouldn't turn around and that the brave lad would keep quiet. She didn't want Kent to see the boy who'd aided in unmasking him, or he might add the child to the list of people he wanted.

From beneath his coat Kent pulled a pistol, aiming it at Miss Lowe. "I've a message for you to take to Lord Borland with Jack Kent's compliments. The viscount is to come to that old ruin of a barn a mile or so back up this road here. He's to come alone. I'll let daylight into this lady if'n I see any face but his." He gestured at Adriana as if there were some doubt whom he meant.

When Miss Lowe stood staring at him in horror, Jack shouted, "Go now, you cursed squeeze crab!"

Miss Naomi Lowe, her face as white as the falling snow, raced down the embankment, then ran shrieking up the path beside the river, the lady's confidence in her abilities equal to a man's in tatters.

William tossed the book on the nearby table, then rose and went to the window of the library. Why couldn't he

concentrate? He'd picked up four books in the last hour
and yet none had held his attention. It was Adriana Addington's fault. All he could think about was her insinuation that he was hiding from his emotions. He wanted
to deny it to himself, yet here he was, alone in his grandmother's library, while most of her guests were out enjoying the coming of Christmas. Was it just a matter of
old habit, or was he deliberately isolating himself?

As his mind wrestled with his thoughts, he gazed out
at the small garden beyond the windows. Suddenly he
took note that the sculpted boxwood trees, which had
been perfectly visible when he'd entered the library, were
becoming completely covered in snow. The storm appeared to be increasing.

At that moment he heard sounds of one of the parties
returning from their mission. Curious, he went to the
library door and saw Baxter directing the footmen as
they carried the heavy Yule Log into the Queen's Drawing Room. His gaze quickly scanned the crowd of ladies
and gentlemen removing their wraps and realized that
Adriana had chosen instead to go to the river.

On impulse, William exited the library. He was tired
of all this soul searching. He needed to remember that
Christmas was a joyous holiday. He would go out and
get some air. He asked a footman to have a horse saddled
and ready for him in ten minutes. Then he hurried to his
room to retrieve his greatcoat and hat, determined to go
help those who'd chosen to cut the greenery.

The black gelding he always rode awaited him at the
open front door. Baxter stood at his post. "You are going
out in this weather, my lord?"

"I thought I would. Mayhap I shall join the others at
the river. The weather is getting worse, and no doubt they
could use an extra pair of hands. I shall never understand
why Grandmother waits until Christmas Eve to do all
the cuttings."

" 'Tis bad luck to have holly in the house before then, my lord." Baxter seemed surprised that his lordship wasn't aware of such.

William, rarely paying heed to superstitions, merely snorted as he drew on his York tan gloves. It was his belief such nonsense was obeyed only by the uninformed. He mounted and rode in the direction of the river. The tracks made by the sledge's runners were almost completely gone but not quite. He followed along at a safe pace, not wanting to injure the horse in the deepening snow.

On reaching the rise, he found the sledge half full of greenery. Below, through the swirling flakes, the viscount could see footmen and women busily at work with shears, but there didn't seem to be very many ladies. He dismounted, tying the horse to the sledge, and started down the hill.

Suddenly from his left a woman came stumbling up a path from the south, crying for someone to help her. Her poke bonnet had fallen from her head, exposing blonde tresses. He recognized the avowed bluestocking looking anything but confident.

William dashed to the distressed woman, as did others near the trees, but he reached her first. He grabbed her shoulders, trying to steady her. "What has happened, Miss Lowe?"

She turned a tearstained face to him even as the footmen, Miss Patton, and Lady Peters crowded around. "My lord, a monstrous brute came along the road and has taken Miss Addington captive."

The viscount's heart seemed to miss a beat, then it began to race in his chest. "Who took her and where?"

The nearly hysterical woman shook her head. "He said his name was Jack Kent and that he knew you both. He was very emphatic that he wants you to come for her alone. If he sees anyone else, he's threatened to kill her."

William's gut knotted with those words. He couldn't even think about Adriana being dead, or his mind wouldn't function properly. Instead, he pushed the black thought aside and centered his anger on Sir Perrick's dastardly half brother. For years he'd known the man for the bad seed he was. Now it seemed Kent wanted to exact a little revenge on both him and Adriana for at last being brought to justice.

"Where did he take her?"

"He said the abandoned barn that sits back from the road to Kelso, just beyond the bridge. He's waiting for you there."

William turned to one of the footmen he recognized. "Bert, make certain that all the women are taken safely back to the castle, then have Baxter unlock the gun room and arm yourselves. Bring a carriage to the bridge Miss Lowe mentioned. Make certain to stay out of sight until you are summoned."

"Very good, my lord."

About to leave, William was delayed when Naomi Lowe clutched at his sleeves. "My lord, your little footman disappeared into the woods, looking for mistletoe. He never returned when the villain arrived. I don't know what happened to him, but no doubt he fled to save himself."

Knowing Nick, the viscount very much doubted that. "I shall find him as well. Now, go with Bert, all of you."

Without a backward glance, William hurried up the path where Miss Lowe just returned. He arrived at the bridge some minutes later and climbed the fence.

Almost at once he spied Nick's small footprints in the snow, gamely following after Kent's horse. The prints were rapidly filling with snow.

"Foolish boy, he'll get himself killed." But he knew he admired that lad's spunk and loyalty.

The viscount had gone over a mile when, through the

swirling whiteness, he could make out the crumbled remains of the abandoned barn sitting back from the road. He stopped to survey Kent's position. William knew the odds were stacked against him. He had no weapon nor any element of surprise, since Kent knew he would come. How was he going to save Adriana?

A movement to his left drew his eye. Nick peered out from behind a large granite rock, motioning for William to come. He went to the boy and crouched low behind the boulder.

"I knew ye'd come for Miss Addington. That 'ighwayman's got 'er in that old buildin'. I done circled the place, and there's a 'ole in the back. Maybe we can sneak in and—"

William shook his head. "He's expecting me, that won't work."

"What's yer plan, m'lord?"

The viscount's mind raced. He had to get Adriana free. He'd known from the moment he'd heard she'd been abducted that he couldn't live without her. He gazed over the top of the rock that hid them. In truth, there was only one thing he could do. Adriana was inside, and she needed him.

"I'm going in, Nick."

The lad's gaze grew wide. "Where's yer barkin' iron?"

"I'm not armed, but here is what you must do."

Nick listened, nodding all the while. When his lordship finished telling him the plan, the boy had his doubts it would work. After all, he'd never seen his lordship lift anything heavier than a book. When his gaze locked with Lord Borland's blue eyes, Nick saw a steely determination that convinced him that all would be well.

The old barn smelled of mildewed hay and manure, but Adriana paid little heed to the unpleasant odors. Her mind was nearly frozen with fear. Would the viscount merely be coming to his own death if he came to help her? She closed her eyes, knowing she must think of something. What if she could escape? She opened her eyes and scanned the dark interior of the barn.

Her gaze went to Jack Kent, who stood hiding behind the barn door, which hung askew, as he searched the trees for movement. The other door was missing completely, giving Adriana a limited view of the outside, but the falling snow hindered what she could see. There was a taut anticipation in Jack's stance. Clearly, the man was looking forward to what he was about to do to them. The thought frightened her even more. The villain was mad for revenge. Adriana knew she had to escape him before the viscount came, but how?

She again looked around the interior of the ancient building now that her eyes were more adjusted to the darkness. Then she saw a section near the back where the stones had crumbled, leaving an opening. The space was small, but she felt certain she could make her way out. Her hands were tied with a strip of leather Kent had found in the barn, but not her feet. After one last glance to make certain he was looking elsewhere, she rose and dashed for the escape route. But within seconds Kent was beside her. He grabbed her arm, spinning her around.

"Where are ye going, little lady? I ain't finish my business with ye, my pretty."

The man roughly pulled her into his arms, trying to give her a kiss. He smelled unwashed and stinking of gin. Adriana struggled against him in terror. She kicked with her foot and found his shin. Angrily, Jack shoved her into a pile of old hay as he bent to rub the wound.

"Be careful, woman, or I'll kill you afore I 'as me fun with you." He straightened and laughed at the horror evident on the lady's face. Then he sobered and took a step toward Adriana.

"Get away from her, Kent!" The words echoed in the empty barn with a quiet but deadly menace. Kent turned to see Lord Borland standing just inside the barn.

Adriana didn't know whether she should cry for joy at the sight of the viscount or weep at the fact that his arms hung at his sides with clenched fists, weaponless. Were they doomed? Was she to be ravished by the villain after his lordship lay dead?

"Ah, so the mighty Lord Borland has come to save the lady. How noble. I must say, 'tis been a puzzle to me why ye've been so determined to see me in the goal even afore I robbed you. But it don't make no difference now, my lord. I've decided to put an end to your interferin' in me affairs afore I sail away from this wretched island."

William advanced on the man. "Let Miss Addington go. She had nothing to do with your being arrested."

"Didn't she now? But the constable said she and that whelp from the coach bleated to Kingston it was me." Jack, holding his pistol aimed at Borland's heart, seemed to strike a thoughtful pose. "Reckon I ought to find that little demon and put a hole in him too. But I ain't got the time. Me ship sails from Liverpool within a week. Just time enough to exact a little revenge on ye two."

The man's eyes glowed with malice. He cocked the pistol, but just at that moment a thumping sound came at the back of the barn. Jack turned to see if the woman was again trying to escape. A blond-headed imp peered through the small opening in the wall.

While Kent was distracted, William lunged forward, brushing the pistol aside. Kent turned back to defend himself, but the viscount threw a handful of sawdust he held in his clenched fist. The man's eyes burning, he stumbled, and the gun fired harmlessly into the air. William planted a facer that would have made Gentleman Jackson proud, knocking the highwayman to the ground.

In an instant, his lordship was on the fellow, pummeling him into submission.

His rage spent, William stopped his assault. He stood, realizing the man was incapable of doing any more harm on this occasion. His lordship's gaze shifted to Adriana, who still lay in the hay, watching him with wide, brown eyes.

Nick appeared at his side with several links of rope he'd found. "Ye got 'im, m'lord. I'll tie 'im up and you go 'elp Miss Addington to 'er feet."

William merely nodded, not needing the boy to tell him to go to the woman he realized he couldn't live without. He knelt beside her, taking her in his arms. "Are you unhurt, my love?"

Adriana thought she must be dreaming, but she melted into his arms, her head against his chest. "I was so frightened but I'm unharmed. You were utterly wonderful."

He lifted her chin and without another word kissed her trembling lips with a gentleness that grew to hunger. At last they parted, breathless, gazing into each other's eyes.

In a hoarse whisper, William said, "Do you think you could love someone who has been a complete and utter fool, my beautiful Adriana?"

"No, my lord, but I could love you madly and I do."

The viscount laughed and crushed her to him. At that moment nothing else mattered in the world.

Behind them, Nick asked, "What's so funny?"

William rose, helping Adriana to her feet, then happily put an arm around her waist as they turned to the boy, who'd finished tying up Jack Kent.

"Life, dear boy. Just when you think you have it all under control, it surprises you."

Nick grinned. "I love surprises."

"Then stick with us, lad, for I suspect our lives shall be one unanticipated event after another." The viscount gazed into Adriana's eyes with such intensity, she blushed, then leaned her head against his shoulder.

Ever the quick one, Nick put his arms akimbo and tilted his head. "Are the pair of ye gettin' buckled?"

Lifting Adriana's chin, William said, "If the lady will have me? Will you marry me, my love?"

"Are you sure, my lord? I am a troublesome creature sure to disrupt your life."

"According to my grandmother, it's been a boring life that needs disrupting, and I have come to agree with her. You once told me that you wanted to travel and see the world. I think it's time I learned of the world from other than a book. I should like nothing more than to share my life with you."

"Then I accept, darling Will."

About to embrace her again, the viscount remembered the ever-observant Nick. "Go to the bridge and await the footmen, who should be coming any moment. Signal them to come in and take this brigand to the castle."

Nick saluted, then dashed out into the snow, not caring that his uniform was getting covered with flakes. Miss Addington was going to live with him and the viscount, and the boy was delighted.

For the next thirty minutes Lord Borland and Miss Addington were oblivious of the rest of the world, even the unconscious man at their feet. Finally Nick's shouting informed them the footmen had arrived. Jack Kent was quickly lifted and hauled away to the castle icehouse, where he would remain until the magistrate could be summoned. Adriana and Will rode back to the castle in the coach the footmen had brought, scarcely paying attention to their surroundings.

At Wother Castle, Lady Margaret stood anxiously at the front windows of the Queen's Drawing Room. On seeing the coach rumble up the drive, the lady hurried to the front doors. She waited impatiently, then embraced her grandson and Adriana moments after they stepped down.

"I was so worried when Bert told us what had happened. You are both safe and unharmed?"

"We are fine, Grandmother."

There was something in her grandson's tone that didn't seem quite normal. She eyed him a moment, then looked at Adriana. They both seemed to be withholding some secret. Fearing that something dreadful had occurred during the abduction, she stepped forward and in a lowered voice said, "Tell me the worst."

William couldn't contain his joy. "You may wish us happy, dear Grandmother."

A smile lit the old woman's face, and she immediately hugged her grandson. "I knew you would be perfect for each other. This is marvelous." She kissed Adriana and said all that was proper.

Before anyone could say a word, the countess added, "We must have the wedding on Christmas Day. That will be perfect indeed."

William laughed. "Grandmother, I'm glad you're delighted but I haven't a license nor have the banns been read." He gazed down at Adriana with such a look, the lady blushed. "While I have no objection to a speedy ceremony, 'tis unfortunate, but we shall have to await the legalities for a proper wedding."

"Rubbish, my boy. Do you not think I have thoroughly considered the matter? Why do you think I invited the bishop from your parish? He can write a license at once."

"Why, knowing you, one could only assume you were matchmaking for the Lord Bishop and Miss Patton," William teased.

An arrested expression settled on the countess's face, causing the viscount to say, "Don't even think about such a plot, Grandmother. Leave the man alone. You have a wedding to help plan. There is no time to be interfering in anyone else's affairs."

"True, my dear boy."

Lady Margaret was all aflutter as she rushed her grandson and soon-to-be granddaughter into the castle. After a warming cup of tea, which gave the viscount and Adriana time to assure all in the greenery-cutting party they were unharmed, her ladyship whisked the young lady upstairs to take her measurements. The news of the impending nuptials rushed through the guests, which only added to the excitement of the holidays.

So it was that on Christmas Day in the year of 1815, William Jamison, Viscount Borland, wed Miss Adriana Addington in front of a lit Christmas tree, a roaring Yule Log and her ladyship's guests in the Queen's Drawing Room at Wother Castle. The bride looked lovely and the groom handsome. Few of the guests knew that two maids and the castle seamstress had been up most of the night, sewing the yards of lace on the young lady's only white gown. The countess declared that a wedding dress without lace would be shabby, and everyone knew that the Countess of Wotherford never did anything by half.

Epilogue

Adriana stood in front of the mirror in the large chamber she'd been shown to after the wedding celebration. There was such happiness in her heart, she didn't want to remove the gown that Nancy and the others had worked on so hard, but she knew that Will would be there soon. The very thought of his kisses made the blood race in her veins.

As she was about to turn to ring for a maid, the candlelight reflected off the good luck charm she still wore. She reached up and removed it, smiling to think that Alexander's gift had worked its magic. It seemed the charm was lucky. She must send it to Amy at once.

Within minutes, she'd written to give her sister the news of her marriage with a promise that after the honeymoon they would come for Amy. Adriana hoped her sister would enjoy the Season with her cousin, since it would be months before she and her husband returned from abroad. She sealed the good luck charm inside the letter, hoping it would be equally as lucky for Amy, and addressed the outside, then rang for Nancy.

Upon the maid's arrival, Lady Borland handed her the letter. "You must see that this is posted on the morrow."

Nancy pocketed the missive. "And so I will, my lady, but we must remove that gown and have you ready for bed when his lordship arrives."

Adriana blushed but knew she was eager for her husband to arrive. She allowed the maid to help her into a beautiful cream lace nightrail that the countess had gifted her with that morning.

Some ten minutes later, when Will entered the room dressed in his blue brocade dressing gown, Adriana stepped into his arms and whispered, *"Ti voglio tanto bene."*

The viscount traced a finger over her lovely lips. "Which means?"

"I love you very much." Her eyes were dark pools of emotion in the firelight.

He kissed her deeply, then lifted his head to grin at her breathlessly. "You must allow me to have one last book so I may learn Italian."

"You may have as many great tomes as you like, but a language book is one you won't need, for you shall have me always at your side to teach you the words."

In the next moments the newly married lovers found there was no need for words in English or Italian on that wonderful night.

Dear Reader,

One of my first trips abroad was to the Eternal City, Rome. With those fond memories, I wrote THE CHRISTMAS CHARM. If you enjoyed Adriana's and William's romance, look for THE VALENTINE CHARM in February 2001. The trilogy continues with Amy Addington's new life as companion to her cousin, but she finds herself drawn into the hunt for a thief by Sir Hartley Ross in the glittering ballrooms of Bath. Then in April 2001, the Addington trilogy concludes with THE WEDDING CHARM and Major Alexander Addington's return to England. Alexander inherits a title, but discovers that his estate is overrun with smugglers. Is his aunt's ward, the enticing Miss Valara Rochelle, involved as well?

I love to hear from readers and hope you will visit my website at: www.lynncollum.com, or write to me at: P.O. Box 478, DeLand, FL 32721.

With regards,
Lynn Collum

Merlin's Legacy

A Series From
Quinn Taylor Evans

__**Daughter of Fire** $5.50US/$7.00CAN
　　0-8217-6052-1

__**Daughter of the Mist** $5.50US/$7.00CAN
　　0-8217-6050-5

__**Daughter of Light** $5.50US/$7.00CAN
　　0-8217-6051-3

__**Dawn of Camelot** $5.50US/$7.00CAN
　　0-8217-6028-9

__**Shadows of Camelot** $5.50US/$7.00CAN
　　0-8217-5760-1

Call toll free **1-888-345-BOOK** to order by phone or use this coupon to order by mail.

Name _____

Address _____

City _____ State _____ Zip _____

Please send me the books I have checked above.

I am enclosing $_____

Plus postage and handling* $_____

Sales tax (in New York and Tennessee) $_____

Total amount enclosed $_____

*Add $2.50 for the first book and $.50 for each additional book.

Send check or money order (no cash or CODs) to:

Kensington Publishing Corp., 850 Third Avenue, New York, NY 10022

Prices and Numbers subject to change without notice.

All orders subject to availability.

Check out our website at **www.kensingtonbooks.com**

Put a Little Romance in Your Life With
Jo Goodman

__**Crystal Passion** $5.50US/$7.00CAN
    0-8217-6308-3

__**Always in My Dreams** $5.50US/$7.00CAN
    0-8217-5619-2

__**The Captain's Lady** $5.99US/$7.50CAN
    0-8217-5948-5

__**My Reckless Heart** $5.99US/$7.50CAN
    0-8217-45843-8

__**My Steadfast Heart** $5.99US/$7.50CAN
    0-8217-6157-9

__**Only in My Arms** $5.99US/$7.50CAN
    0-8217-5346-0

__**With All My Heart** $5.99US/$7.50CAN
    0-8217-6145-5

Put a Little Romance in Your Life With
Shannon Drake

__Come The Morning	0-8217-6471-3	$6.99US/$8.50CAN
__Conquer The Night	0-8217-6639-2	$6.99US/$8.50CAN
__The King's Pleasure	0-8217-5857-8	$6.50US/$8.00CAN
__Lie Down In Roses	0-8217-4749-0	$5.99US/$6.99CAN
__Tomorrow Glory	0-7860-0021-X	$5.99US/$6.99CAN

Put a Little Romance in Your Life With
Hannah Howell